Ans	_____	M.L.	_____
ASH	_____	MLW	_____
Bev	_____	Mt.Pl	_____
C.C.	_____	NLM	_____
C.P.	_____	Ott	_____
Dick	2/09	PC	_____
DRZ	_____	PH	_____
ECH	_____	P.P.	_____
ECS	_____	Pion.P.	_____
Gar	_____	Q.A.	_____
GRM	02/10 (Peggy)	Riv	_____
GSP	_____	RPP	_____
G.V.	_____	Ross	2/08
Har	_____	S.C.	_____
JPCP	_____	St.A.	11/09
KEN	Sver 9/08	St.J	_____
K.L.	7/09 (52my)	St.Joa	_____
K.M.	_____	St.M.	_____
L.H.	_____	Sgt	7/09
LO	_____	T.H.	_____
Lyn	_____	TLLO	_____
L.V.	_____	T.M.	_____
McC	_____	T.T.	_____
McG	_____	Ven	_____
McQ	11/07	Vets	_____
MIL	_____	VP	9/07 (Jolin)
	_____	Wat	_____
	_____	Wed	_____
	_____	WIL	_____
	_____	W.L.	_____

MOMENT OF DECISION

Benita is a dedicated doctor, but when questions about her professional competence arise following a street accident, she starts afresh as general assistant at Beacon House, a Children's Clinic. However, this brings new problems when she is faced with her boyfriend's disapproval, the Clinic's domineering but charismatic Superintendent, and the two disruptive children she befriends . . . and then she becomes the victim of a blackmailer! There are many urgent decisions to make before Benita's future becomes clear.

Books by Mavis Thomas
in the Linford Romance Library:

MAVIS THOMAS

MOMENT OF DECISION

Complete and Unabridged

LINFORD
Leicester

First published in Great Britain in 2006

First Linford Edition
published 2007

Copyright © 2006 by Mavis Thomas

British Library CIP Data

Thomas, Mavis
    Moment of decision.—Large print ed.—
    Linford romance library
    1. Women physicians—Fiction 2. Love stories
    3. Large type books
    I. Title
    823.9'14 [F]

    ISBN 978–1–84617–722–4

Published by
F. A. Thorpe (Publishing)
Anstey, Leicestershire

Set by Words & Graphics Ltd.
Anstey, Leicestershire
Printed and bound in Great Britain by
T. J. International Ltd., Padstow, Cornwall

This book is printed on acid-free paper

1

'Yes, I'd suggest two or three weeks' rest, after you've had such a difficult time. Why not visit your grandfather in Devon? Or find yourself a nice break somewhere abroad, get some sea air and sunshine?'

I sat beside Dr Halliwell's big, tidy desk, where so many patients parked themselves daily to absorb his professional knowledge and fatherly advice. He was the highly respected senior member of the Group Practice, his list always overflowing. The trouble was, he wasn't addressing now a run-of-the-mill sufferer presenting a gippy stomach or sore throat. I was supposed to be a colleague, a competent and qualified doctor in my own right.

Some twelve months ago, my place here had seemed the fulfilment of every hope and ambition — arduous work

1

and long hours, and a door magically labelled Dr. B. Wilde, the achievement of all the years of study and training. Today the dream looked like vanishing in a puff of smoke.

'I just asked you a question, Benita,' the silver-haired, dark-suited man beside me was saying a little more pointedly. 'You don't appear to be listening.'

I was listening! When you were being told by your superior that you were falling down on your job, you listened! I knew Dr Halliwell had been explaining he wasn't asking for my resignation at this stage, not just yet, but things couldn't go on this way. It was disappointing, he said, after the excellent start I had made.

'We're worried about you, my dear,' he insisted. 'I'm worried, and Roger is worried . . .'

He would know, of course, that Roger (the Dr. R. Shepherd whose labelled door was next to mine) was more to me than just a colleague. Probably he even knew that last night

2

we took Roger's sister out to celebrate her birthday. There was little that escaped him.

'I'm sorry.' I found my voice belatedly. 'But Dr Halliwell, I don't want a holiday, sitting around doing nothing. I'd much rather keep on working!'

'That's very laudable. But you do need to rest, and sort out whatever personal problems are interfering with your work.' He made it sound so simple. 'I've arranged cover for you. Just go home and don't worry!'

He got to his feet, and patted my shoulder in an encouraging way. So that was that. You didn't argue with Edward Halliwell.

On my way out I passed the waiting area where the first patients for morning surgery were arriving, parking umbrellas in the stand. Lately, it seemed always to be raining.

It was as though I had left some of myself back there, as though part of me had died this morning. I should have known what was about to happen, but I hadn't guessed, and I was shocked and stricken. Yet through that numbing pain, one clear thought was taking shape. Roger must have known about this! He was second in seniority to Dr Halliwell, and it seemed he had even been consulted, so why hadn't he warned me last night?

Seizing a chance, I nosed out into the traffic to drive wearily homewards through the rain. All these South London roads, houses, gardens, shops, I had come to know like the back of my hand.

Previously I had worked at St Anselm's Hospital, a few miles from here, an ugly Victorian building which became the centre of my life. I had no time left to make friends. My only close family was my grandfather, in his day a distinguished naturalist and writer, his books on flora and fauna still in demand. His Devonshire cottage had always a loving welcome for me.

After I left St Anselm's and began

here at the surgery, everything went so well. Finding my feet in the new environment, finding a small local flat . . . and finding Roger.

He was ten years older, tall and dark, serious-faced, quiet-voiced. In his company I learned to love the beauty of great music that I had never before paused to appreciate. There were pleasant meals at my flat, or shared Sunday family lunches at Roger's home. He lived not far distant with his widowed sister, Julie, and her teenage son, and from the first it seemed I just slotted in as one of the family.

And that was a new and wonderfully warming experience, something I had missed without quite realising it. Always I had driven myself to the limit, with work for an organisation for disabled children sandwiched into any moments of leisure. There was no time to consider personal loneliness until a day came that turned my whole world on its axis.

It had been a nightmare day, just a

few weeks ago: rainy like today, only the rain had seemed unimportant, just a minor nuisance in a demanding schedule. I was driving back from a late emergency visit after a busy day.

Usually, there was never time to be tired. I had to get home and rest and like a robot I steered my car down the steep twisting hill by St Peter's Church, fighting against weariness.

The impact of metal against a living human form was the first thought I had of anyone walking abroad in this weather. After that, for a timeless space there was just nothing. Just driving rain on the window, no other sound.

Terence Stanton was twenty-four-years old. His home was close by, shared with his pregnant teenage wife. An ambulance raced him to St Anselm's. He had never recovered consciousness, the weak flicker of his life kept in being by skilled care and sophisticated equipment.

I was working again within a few days. Officially exonerated from blame, outwardly recovered, I went on working.

But how could I forget, day or long haunted night, the unresponsive form of Terry Stanton? If he died and his young widow gave birth to a fatherless child — or if he lingered on, either way, this was the burden I must carry all my days . . .

'Oh, Doctor, you're back already! Good, there's a couple of messages.'

A voice broke in on my aching thoughts as I opened the door marked *Seven*, on the first-floor landing of the small white-walled block of flats.

'Your phone messenger thingy was on the blink again — making a noise like a scalded cat! So I wrote them down for you,' Mrs Day said importantly. Grey haired and chatty, immensely capable in her apron and orange rubber gloves, she fulfilled 'domestic duties' at one of the other flats, and I had commandeered her for just a few hours a week.

'One of them's urgent, she didn't

give any name,' she was explaining now. 'But it sounded like the same woman who rang last week when the messager was playing up. Just says 'It's personal' and puts the phone down.'

'That's all right, Mrs Day, I'll attend to it . . . ' I stopped short as I saw the second scribbled message. 'What's this, my grandfather — coming here?'

'He's on his way! A surprise visit, he said. Now isn't that nice for you?' She beamed her approval.

At another time such a visit would be a delight. There was nothing I could do. I forced some sort of smile for Mrs Day, and explained I was taking some leave and would let her know my future plans when I knew them myself.

In my bedroom I changed out of this morning's businesslike suit into jeans and a comfortable sweater. I gave a touch to my long, thick, very dark hair coiled up as usual in no-nonsense but quite elegant style.

I picked up my bag and keys, and let myself out again. Barely ten minutes drive away, after skirting the shopping centre, was the quiet backwater of St Peter's Hill, which often of late I had made a detour to avoid. Other times, like today I came here deliberately, to visit Wendy Stanton, whose child might never know its father.

At first, all my contact with her, by phone or in person, had been voluntary. But lately Wendy had begun leaving messages for me. I was coming to dread them, the childlike voice muffling its sobs, on the point of breaking down.

'Oh! — you've got here!' The door opened before I could press the bell. 'I've been waiting, I — I did so hope you'd come.'

'I just got your message. You know I'll help in any way I can.'

'It's so good of you to bother. Only — I did want to ask you about something,' the girl whispered and stood back for me to enter. As always she looked far less than her barely nineteen years, her fair hair falling straight and limp to her shoulders, her small face lit by wide, pale eyes. Incongruous was the swollen bulk of her figure under a floppy washed-out sweatshirt.

I followed on down the narrow hall. The back room had some nice modern furniture. A state-of-the-art television screen completely filled one corner. All tending to the lavish side for the young couple, perhaps.

Which was confirmed as Wendy went on, her voice becoming more and more that of a forlorn child. There were hire purchase payments outstanding, bills to be paid.

'Do you think I should send the things back, Dr Wilde? Would that be best? But, if Terry does wake up next time I see him, he'll be so upset . . . he wanted everything nice for me and the baby . . . '

The brimming eyes overflowed. As always, I clung by deliberate will to numbness, dulling eyes and ears and mind — for otherwise this would be impossible to bear. And I had to bear it!

A framed photograph of Terry Stanton's young, pleasant face watched me in silent accusation.

The girl had to talk to someone. She was so young, she seemed very much alone. It was as though sitting here listening was some sort of atonement I must make.

I advised her gravely, 'Don't make any rushed decisions, Wendy. Wait and see.' Already I had unzipped my bag to extract my cheque book. Today I could sit here no longer in this room.

'Oh, but you did that last week, Dr Wilde — and I can't think when we'll be able to pay it back! But . . . ' She wavered as I waited with my pen poised. 'Perhaps just one more little loan would help such a lot . . . '

I made out the cheque for two hundred pounds and then stood up quickly, waving aside Wendy's thanks. She clambered heavily from her chair to follow me to the door.

Outside, it was still raining. I drove

away quickly from this house, this accursed road. I couldn't drive away from the waking nightmare.

A sober grey car was just leaving The Heights when I got home, and recognition was mutual and immediate. The grey car stopped again, the driver unfurling his tall figure into the rain. Coming straight from the Stanton home, chilled and shaken, this wasn't at all the moment I would have chosen to face Roger Shepherd with his puzzling, painful disloyalty.

'I'm glad I've found you. Nancy Shore said you'd gone home after seeing Halliwell.' I heard his level voice, I felt his hand on my arm. 'I'm so sorry about it. Can we go inside out of this infernal wet?'

I walked with him silently up the stairway. We went into the flat, and I flicked on the electric fire that looked like glowing logs, lighting the cushioned sofas.

The confused numbness of shock left me suddenly, my thoughts were sharp and clear. All his concern for me was just a little late!

'Roger, you knew about it! Dr Halliwell asked your opinion, didn't he?'

He hesitated momentarily and frowned.

'You knew I'd be shown the door this morning! Even if you couldn't persuade him not to do it, at least you could have warned me!' My voice rose as belated anger and humiliation boiled over. 'You let me walk in there and gape at him like — like a stranded fish! I suppose you didn't want to step out of line with the Big Chief, was that it? Well, was it?'

'At least let's get our facts right.' The quiet of his voice was a rebuke in itself. 'You were not shown the door.'

'Wasn't I? I know I've made mistakes lately, but I'm not wholly stupid! Isn't it obvious if I don't resign very quickly he'll ask me to go?'

He sat down on the arm of the settee, still betraying no reaction of anger. That considered calm of his was seldom ruffled. Maybe it gave reassurance at anxious sickbeds, but to my pain and bitterness now it was no comfort.

'Well,' I plunged on, 'you're both well rid of me! Give me a minute to write out my resignation and you can deliver it to him in person! And you'll both be pleased to know it will be a permanent resignation.' I was calmer now, quite deliberate. 'As from today, Doctor Wilde reverts to plain Miss! If I haven't given full attention to the job, let down the patients, that's unforgivable and that's what I have to do! I suppose I should be grateful to Halliwell, he helped me to — to find myself out.'

If I expected amazement, warm protests, they didn't come. The calm of this man was a little unnerving sometimes. But maybe it was only an outward cover. He removed his gold-rimmed glasses and began carefully polishing the lenses. Without them, the pale, high-browed face looked younger.

'I was afraid of an extreme reaction like this. I warned him you'd take it badly, you've been under such a strain lately.'

'Nice of you!' I muttered.

'Benita, I don't need to tell you, we hold a brief of supreme responsibility. I had to agree with him, you've been driving yourself too hard — you do badly need a break, a good rest. Goodness knows that business with young Stanton was enough to unsettle anyone.'

In another fifteen, twenty years of steady, patient service, Roger Shepherd would be another Ernest Halliwell, equally revered and respected. Well, so be it. The world had sore need of them.

He unloosed my tightly clenched hand — and went on holding it.

'Will you do something for me?' he was asking. 'Postpone your decision, just get right away from here for a spell? Devon with your granddad would be ideal. Though of course — I'll miss you.'

I said quietly, 'How can I go off on holiday when the Stantons . . . '

'The Stantons.' He frowned just perceptibly. 'They're the main reason you should go. I've told you before, you're getting far too emotionally involved.'

It could have been Dr Halliwell saying that. Except, could you really picture him, even in his distant youth, balanced on a settee-arm holding a girl's hand?

'Look at the thing in perspective, Benita. You don't remember what happened, you're torturing yourself with guilt, but there's no reason to do that! You're an experienced and competent driver, obviously you did everything possible to avoid that boy. He must have blundered out in front of you, so blaming yourself won't help anyone or solve anything, will it?'

I turned my head away. Always he gave logical, reasonable advice, and this was some more. Write off the stricken life of a stranger as someone else's tragedy.

'Come on, now.' I heard his voice

close to me. 'I'm sorry I must rush away, I'm running very late . . . But will you think seriously about what I've said?'

I promised I would. That at least I could do.

When he was gone, I went on sitting there. I could still feel the parting touch of his lips on mine. The flat was very quiet and very empty.

★　★　★

It didn't stay empty for long. Bradley Wilde had made good time from Devon. The trains were running well and he managed to get a taxi immediately, he said.

I put up my face for his customary warm kiss as I ushered him through to the fireside. He was well into his late seventies, but still a fine upstanding figure, the craggy bearded face lighted by undimmed slate-grey eyes.

For a number of years, after accident and illness robbed me of both my

17

parents in quick tragic succession, he had accommodated his life and his windower's home to a grieving child's loneliness. Suddenly it was all I could do now not to break down and seek solace in his strong arms.

'I suppose you're up to your eyes as usual,' he was saying. 'But if you can manage some free time while I'm here, there's something I'd like us to do together, I'll explain it presently. That's partly why I've descended on you out of the blue!'

'I'm sure I can manage that,' I agreed. Pouring him a mug of the strong, scalding tea he imbibed by the gallon, I joined him on the sofa, very aware of that searching gaze of his.

'I can see you're still overworking. And there's no better news of young Stanton? No, you'd have told me. You know, you've really got me worried! That last chat we had on the phone, your last letter — well, that's another reason why I'm here. The Stanton affair must have been the final straw, but even before that I felt things weren't quite right with you. Why not write off this year as experience and make a fresh start somewhere? Maybe a nice little vacation first?'

'I'm on a sort of vacation already. A couple of weeks 'to think things over' . . . but there's no more thinking to do.' I took a deep breath. 'I'm handing in my resignation to Dr Halliwell. Not just that, I'm leaving medicine for good!'

I hated to deliver this blow that would be so devastating to him. For a moment he had no answer, utterly amazed.

'Bennie.' The pet name for that bereft child long ago, that was always gentle and loving on his lips. 'Bennie, this is foolish talk. You're obviously not yourself just now.'

'I'm quite myself, I know what I'm doing. Oh, you don't want a catalogue of the mistakes I've made, I know I'm a liability to the profession! I've just been explaining it all to Roger.'

'You've talked to Roger? If he didn't

tell you you're crazy, he has less sense than I thought! Look here, no-one is infallible. You're overstressed and over-tired, or you wouldn't entertain such an idea for a moment!'

'Grandad, it's not the end of the world. Let's forget it for now.' It seemed his strong face had aged in just a moment.

He explained then the reason for his flying visit to London. It seemed he had recently met an old friend at some sort of reunion lunch: Edgar Dwyer had especially asked him to seek my advice for another friend, who was Superin-tendent of the Beacon House Clinic situated down near the Sussex coast.

'I've never heard of it,' I said a little guardedly. 'Beacon?'

'Beacon. I suppose, because it's intended to light the way ahead? Eddie's friend isn't just in charge, he founded the place.'

Its aims were centred, he explained, on the early salvation of children in need of specialised help. Sometimes the neglected, sometimes juvenile drop-outs or misfits or rebels, but always the uncooperative, the downright unmanageable. All capable of being transformed into useful citizens.

'Beacon House is a pilot scheme, to prove what might be done on a larger scale — that's if it proves anything. I gather they're living on borrowed time, this Superintendent fellow is running things almost single-handed. He told Eddie if his grant isn't renewed, which is touch and go, he'll have to shut up shop anyway.'

I refrained from saying I was scarcely surprised. 'But what exactly does Mr Dwyer think I can do about it?' I asked reasonably.

'Ah, this is the point. He knows my granddaughter is . . . hem! . . . an up-and-coming young doctor, and you have connections with disabled children's organisations. He thought you could possibly recommend someone rash enough to fill a vacancy at Beacon House and help to keep it running. I said I'd ask you.'

'I'm sorry, I don't know anyone quite as rash as that!' I said uneasily.

No, I almost cried aloud. NO! Haven't I problems enough, without adding Beacon House to the list?

Bradley Wilde was doing his loving, caring best for me. He supposed new work, new faces, a whole fresh incentive, would shake all sorts of foolish notions out of my system. Which meant he didn't understand, any more than Roger understood, that the all-efficient Dr Wilde had been just a myth.

I said if I *could* think of some misguided soul to recommend for the vacancy, I would tell him. His disapproving glance spoke volumes.

★　★　★

'No change,' was the report from the hospital when I rang. I carried those sombre tidings to my restless pillow. Very early next morning I was astir again.

My grandfather had already vacated his resting place on the 'convertible' sofa in the lounge to brew up tea in the small kitchen. As he surveyed me, I knew the fact that I hadn't slept was dismally obvious.

In a while I served up toast and eggs and tomatoes, and we sat together at the table. It seemed to me we were like two cagey chess players, each waiting for the other to come up with a move.

'Look here, my dear!' He pushed aside his plate suddenly. 'This just won't do! I know it's no use telling you to book a cruise to the Med! And taking you back to Devon wouldn't do much for either of us. But the rain has stopped, we both have a free day — how about a nice drive in the countryside to blow away the cobwebs?'

'You mean the Sussex countryside, of course?' I hinted.

I had to comply. If he really wanted to go, that alone made the trip worthwhile.

From my bedroom I heard his voice

on the telephone. 'Beacon House? Good! I'd like a word with the Superintendent if . . . ah, yes, good morning, sir! You don't know me, but we have a mutual friend, Edgar Dwyer? Yes, well, he was telling me about your staffing problems. I wondered if I might bring my granddaughter along to see you . . . '

Even from a distance I could hear a child shouting shrilly at the Beacon House end. The place sounded like Bedlam! Unfortunately, it didn't seem to deter my Grandfather. In a short while I was unlocking my car.

We travelled on South, away from London, presently in pleasant sunshine. Bypassing the clustered high-rise blocks of busy Croydon we hummed along the main route towards Brighton.

At least the air here was fresh, partly denuded trees stood russet and gold against glimmers of blue sky. The village turned out to be a sprawl of houses around a main street, boasting a closed-up railway station, a square with a War Memorial, and a bus-stand.

A long puddle-strewn lane, leading off beside the picturesquely-timbered Three Doves hostelry, brought us to a length of high green-painted railings, obviously enclosing the grounds of some large house. A short distance more produced a tall iron gate with a brass nameplate: Beacon House Residential Clinic.

I got out to unfasten the gate, and again on the other side to refasten it. Grimly I commented, 'Pretty poor security arrangements!'

The house, an extensive creeper-clad ramble of weathered old brick and pointed gables, had been much patched and painted up. Most of the higher windows, doubtless bedrooms or dormitories, had wooden slats across them: possibly against accidents — or conceivably midnight escape plans with bed-sheet ropes?

I rang the bell, and then rang it again. We went on waiting in a glass outer porch graced by assorted ailing pot-plants and mud-plastered trainers.

I was just ringing again when the door was opened by a domestic helper with peroxide hair and a sour face, evidently in a state of muttering ill humour. 'Can't be in two places at once, can I? One pair of hands, that's all I've got! Yes? Well? Parents, are you? Or more of them council people about the drains?'

'We're neither. The Superintendent is expecting us,' I assured her.

'Is he? Well, he's busy with the new little kid. Can you come back later?'

'I don't think so!' My determination was rising. 'Could I see anyone else?'

'Matron's off sick. Has been for weeks. And Miss Price is out.'

'Then we'll have to come inside and wait, won't we?'

Grudgingly, the door was opened wider — exuding an aroma which identified itself instantly in my mind. School dinners!

'Thanks, if you'd just tell the Superintendent Benita Wilde is here?' I requested. 'And is it all right to make a phone call while I'm here?' Like a complete fool, I had left my mobile sitting beside my bed.

Our guide nodded towards a pay-phone out in the hall area. 'You can try. If them little perishers haven't jammed it up with chewing gum again. All right, I'll tell Dr Lowery. Get me head bit off again, I daresay.'

I tapped out my home number. Carefully I had shut the waiting room door behind me, because of the so difficult secrets I was keeping. 'Mrs Day! Oh good, I'm so glad I caught you!'

'Nothing from the hospital, or Dr Shepherd. But someone did call just now,' Mrs Day reported importantly. 'Private, no name, but I got a number from him. A man with quite a stammer, it was. Very important, he said, and you need to ring him back.'

It was a London number. Some patient recommended to me, perhaps? Then why hadn't they called the surgery?

This time I was answered, surprisingly, 'Pete's Diner here!'

'Good grief! Who did you say?'

'We're a café, love. Name of Wilde, is it?'

'Well! Yes, it is! I had a message . . . '

'That's right. Young bloke here wants you. All yours!' the laconic voice called to someone. There was some delay, then another voice came on the line, low spoken, hard to follow against the background of chatter and clattering crockery.

'Good afternoon. I had to talk to you, there's something we ought to d-discuss. A man was hurt in a street accident recently, badly hurt . . . very b-badly hurt . . . '

'Who are you?' A chill unreality was beginning to possess me.

'I'm no-one special. But I was there, when it happened. I — I s-saw it all . . . '

'All right, if you were there,' I demanded, 'why haven't you come forward before?'

'I didn't want to get involved — p-personal reasons, but it bothers me, you see. I can't let you get away with it. Not when there's a man d-dying by inches . . . '

I rummaged desperately for another coin, and failed to find one. I babbled, 'Wait, I've no more money, I've got to know who you are! You'll have to ring me back.'

'I can't now. Not now. Another d-day . . . '

He was gone. There was nothing but whirling nightmare that spun the world all about me, that turned my own racing heartbeats into deafening hammer-blows. For days I had scarcely eaten or slept. I had no strength to fight off this new horror.

The floor was coming up to meet me. There was nothing I could do to stop it.

2

'Whoops!' a voice said. I was just aware, as I swayed and stumbled, that someone had run downstairs to catch me. I was being held, like the day in far off childhood when I fell out of a tree-house my grandfather had built. But they weren't his arms holding me now.

I blinked at a stranger's face. Eyes of an unusually vivid blue looked straight back at me from a galaxy of freckles. 'Are you back with us? Don't look so worried, Beacon House usually takes days rather than minutes to floor people, but there has to be a first time!'

It was annoying that my introduction to Clive Lowery had turned out so very undignified. 'I'm sorry, I'll be all right now.' I fought back remaining clouds of faintness. 'I've been under rather a strain lately.'

'Overwork? Tell me about it!'

'I really shouldn't have come here. And I ought to get back to London right away, there's something very urgent.'

'You're not going anywhere just yet.' His smile was bright and disarming, but the suddenly authoritative tone brooked no argument. Still without releasing my arm, he pushed open a neighbouring door. 'My office. That big chair, I think — just take it slowly. Make yourself at home.'

'But I can't . . . ' I started again. I got no farther, suddenly finding myself lodged in the big cushioned chair. He was picking up a telephone on his desk.

'Elsie? Look, I know you're up to your lilywhite elbows in lunches, but can you manage tea and sandwiches in my office for two visitors?'

Still rebellious, I was finding my surroundings hadn't quite stopped spinning around me. The man was infuriatingly right in making me stay, of course. And really there was no point in rushing madly back to London.

With rising curiosity, I was taking stock of the room. Bay-windowed and carpeted, it was more of a homely sitting-room than an office. There was the desk and a filling cabinet, a somewhat ancient-looking computer with sticky notes haphazardly framing the screen, but a table was covered with crayons and paper and an uncompleted jigsaw puzzle. A corner of the desk was occupied by a loudly snoring black cat with very ragged ears, which opened baleful green eyes to observe me.

'Smiler,' Dr Lowery said. 'If he keeps on sleeping in my 'in' tray, one day Miss Price will file him away under 'S'.'

As my attention turned back to the man at the desk, for some reason I started wondering how old he was. Possibly mid-thirties, perhaps more, certainly older than he looked at first glance. It was quite an ordinary face, one you wouldn't notice in a crowd. That blue-eyed smile, of course, was something else. Not strictly blue, not as green as smiler's, maybe a rare and mesmerising shade of turquoise?

Suddenly conscious of staring, I apologised tersely, 'I'm sorry to be a nuisance! I'm afraid I'm not really interested in working here — '

'I know. Oh, most people have reservations about Beacon House. But I do badly need extra help. You're experienced with children, so I want you to have a look round. We might just find you fit in! Don't you agree this is a worthwhile venture?'

'Very worthwhile, in theory. But — '

'But you believe there are good kids and bad kids, and a magic transformation can't be worked on them by high-flown theories? When you feel better, you'll let me show you round? No obligations?'

I was saved the need to reply by an approaching rattle of crockery. He hailed it cheerfully, 'Our Elsie with the tea.'

My grandfather joined us, and for the next twenty minutes I sat there largely silent, listening to the conversation: all very general and impersonal, mostly about their mutual friend, Edgar Dwyer, and his new house.

After that came what our host called *The Grand Tour*. Accompanied by his undeniably entertaining commentary, we saw the spacious dining-room with its red plastic-topped tables and chairs, the classroom area where a visiting teacher presided daily, the activity rooms for various handicrafts, music and games.

Upstairs we glimpsed one of the small, homely dormitories, beds spread with cheery striped covers. Twenty children could be accommodated, but at present there were less, all aged under eleven. Most had been resident for some while.

During our rounds he had needed to check a minor riot on the back stairs and another more serious in the dining-room. There as well, the ubiquitous Elsie was grumbling mightily over the grisly task of scooping somebody's fried egg and baked beans off a wall.

This time the miscreant was the newest resident, arrived only this morning. A sullen-faced beanpole of a child named Kylie Chambers, she was crouched in silent misery and rebellion under a table, defying all comers.

I watched Dr Lowery stoop beside her to whisper, 'Don't worry about it, pet. You know where my room is? Well, when you want to talk, I'll be there.'

In the corridor my Grandfather asked with interest, 'Will she talk to you?'

'Not yet. Eventually, I hope. There'll be a lot of water — or maybe baked beans — to flow under the bridge first.'

For a moment his face was transformed by a depth of gravity I hadn't seen before. 'You see, each one of these mixed-up kids, when they arrive here, is so terribly alone. You can try to teach them no man is an isolated island, every thought or act means joy or pain to those all around. You can occupy the destructive little hands that are trying to fight back. But that's just a start and the price of failure is too great, believe me!'

With a strange sense of discovery I realised he was passionately in earnest. I glanced back at the forlorn, defiant huddle of the child in a sudden new compassion, almost like fellow feeling. I knew what it was like to flounder in a lonely sea of trouble.

Then I heard my name spoken, as my grandfather was telling our guide, 'You and Benita will have things to discuss, so I'll just explore your grounds, if I may?'

'Be my guest. Picturesque mud, every known type of weed.' The Superintendent glanced round at me. 'My office, Doctor?'

This would be the difficult part. Beacon House looked like fulfilling most of my pre-conceived ideas, not a school, not a hospital, but with the worst points of both — and its Head, of course, would be impossible to work with. Yet at this moment I was quite strongly tempted just to rush headlong into this uphill struggle and do my best for Kylie and all the other Kylies.

'Please,' I heard Clive Lowery's plea, 'I do hate to see a lady frown! You really found the place that bad, Dr Wilde?'

'No. I was interested, especially in Kylie. I hope you succeed in what you're trying to do. Although I still wonder . . . '

'You wonder if most of our inmates need a smacked bottom more than fancy behaviour therapy?'

I coughed. 'I didn't say that!'

'No need to. What people don't tell me, I usually figure out for myself.'

'Then you probably know as well there's no point in calling me Doctor Wilde? I've decided to resign permanently from the profession.'

After the pain of telling this to my grandfather and to Roger, there was less trauma in announcing it to a stranger. And the shattering statement didn't shake him as I had expected. He merely said, 'Have you, indeed? I just need an assistant, no real qualifications except being good with the kids. But let's talk about you first.'

He was looking so directly into my face that I felt I was undergoing an X-ray. 'Yes, you, Benita Wilde . . . still a little pale and wan, but those are very fine dark eyes to match the raven hair . . . but they're sad eyes, angry eyes, frightened eyes. Listen to me, footballers hang up their boots, pop singers hang up their tonsils, but only very desperate doctors decide to hang up their stethoscopes!'

I wished now I had kept quiet. I said sharply, 'All right, I'm desperate! Too many mistakes, if you need the lurid details!'

I felt the colour rising in my face. But rescue was at hand, for surely he couldn't continue to ignore a loud disturbance upstairs? What I had mentally christened 'a holiday camp for hooligans' was living up to the title. I couldn't help a grim glimmer of satisfaction.

★ ★ ★

When the door burst open, a young nurse I had seen before, looking younger than ever with her pale-blue uniform tunic askew and her hair a mess, rushed in. Close behind her a noisy group of heads bobbed and weaved, struggling to see what would happen.

Clive Lowery gave his attention to the onlookers first.

'Now then, you lot! Paul — Jackie, Michelle — is that Greg hiding at the back? If you've anything to say to me, step inside!'

The group exchanged glances. They didn't 'step inside': I was a little amazed that they melted away like ice in the sun. Closing the door, he turned to the distressed girl.

'Nurse, what are we going to do with you? How long have you been here now?'

'S-six weeks.'

'Six weeks. And you still don't know

rule one — never panic in front of them? Well, Nurse Graves, lesson learned, I hope. Now let's hear what the trouble is!'

The trouble again was Kylie Chambers. After her lunchtime exploits she had bolted upstairs to a bathroom, somehow jammed the lock, and was in a stage of siege.

Certainly, he wasn't rushing to investigate. I thought with even greater pity of the dark-eyed child who had so caught my attention. This lack of concern boiled up again my anger at his attitude.

'I'm told this is one of her specialities,' he was telling the apprehensive young nurse. 'Not to worry, Annette!'

This time Annette Graves raised her moist and downcast eyes, and the look in them was unmistakable. She adored Dr Lowery.

I asked crisply, 'You don't intend leaving that child up there, I hope. She could injure herself very badly!'

'What would you suggest?'

'Surely this is a cry for help. She doesn't need teaching a lesson, she needs comfort and reassurance. She believes no-one in the wide world understands how she feels! Well, I'd like to try talking to her.'

'You have a try, if you want,' he invited.

At the bathroom door I started explaining gently and encouragingly that everyone here was a friend, nothing here was unkind or frightening, to the unseen Kylie on the other side. Unseen, but the sound of things being thrown around left no doubt of her presence. It took quite a while before she gradually quietened down. There followed gusty breathing and muffled sobs.

'I've only just arrived here too, Kylie,' I persisted. 'It's all new and strange and lonely for me too. But couldn't we give it a chance? Why not open the door so we can talk about it?'

'Well, I can't, can I?' I was answered at last, with half-hearted belligerence. 'I can't get it undone, can I? So now I'll starve.'

'You won't starve, Kylie. I'm sure they'll be able to open the door. I'll stop here with you, I won't go away.'

As proof, I inserted my hand under the door as far as it would go. The gusty breathing sounded still gustier. I felt a thrill of strangely warming joy when small fingers touched the tip of mine, and stayed touching them.

Only a tiny victory, of course. But that sense of joy remained with me all the while a 'rescue operation' was put into effect. It wasn't long before there were sounds of sawing, hammering and scrambling: 'A funny little man coming in the window,' Kylie confided. In a few minutes more the door was opened by a small, elderly man in faded overalls, whose face bore a rather striking resemblance to a monkey. I guessed he was the maintenance-cum-handyman of the establishment.

The child was sobbing again now, and I held her gently, silently, till the tide of emotion ebbed a little. Then, as all the onlookers had been dispersed, I was able to escort her quietly along to the sick-bay, a room I had noted on the *Grand Tour*.

Outside on the grass some sort of ball game was taking place, and I let Kylie watch through the window while I bathed her hot damp face and some minor bruises. The dismal sniffing subsided gradually.

She looked at me a little less sullenly. She wasn't a pretty child, her tautly thin face sharp featured, her dark eyes narrowed in resentment. But I saw them turn with another spark of interest to a cupboard spilling out a muddle of books and games, and a half-bald teenage doll in bedraggled ball gown finery, stuffed in head first.

'Do you want her? No-one else does, by the look of her! No? Oh well, I'll throw her in the bin when I go downstairs.'

I covered up the huddled form on the bed, sat down and feigned sleep. Under lowered lids I watched Kylie stir, glance at me suspiciously, then make a grab for the neglected doll. It vanished quickly under her plaid rug.

Perhaps five minutes later, low regular breathing told me it was safe to move. I tiptoed to the door, and then almost let out a cry of surprise. I wondered how long Clive Lowery had been a silent witness.

He put a finger to his lips until we were along the landing. 'Well done! I could hardly have managed that better myself.'

More of his infuriating arrogance! But he had something else to say, as we walked back towards his office.

'Yes, you handled it like a dream, you're a natural! So I'm offering you a job here. How do you feel about it?'

I hesitated, remembering that difficult interview with him a while ago. It was unnerving to have my thoughts read yet again.

'I know! I wasn't too impressed with you at first, was I? Frankly, I was a bit worried about your opinion of Beacon House rubbing off on the kids. But I gave you the chance to cope with Kylie, and you've changed my mind. Say, a fortnight's trial run, no lasting commitments yet on either side?'

A fortnight. Just a fortnight out of my tangled life in London. Would that matter so much? Might not a short spell here clear my mind so I could see those troubles more distinctly? I could remain in close touch with Wendy, and with Roger. As for my own sad ineptitude, surely I could do no harm here in just two weeks.

I asked, 'Can I let you know definitely tomorrow?'

It was high time to be starting on the drive back. 'You'll ring me, then?' Clive Lowery was saying. 'Start as soon as you like. Of course, there are references et cetera, but I do take a relaxed view of paperwork . . . '

Another small car had just slid in beside mine, and its driver was starting to unload bags and parcels. She was a small, slight girl of maybe mid-twenties, whose curly dark hair framed a round, attractive face. There was a natural grace in her movements, and in the way a fly-away silk scarf was knotted at her throat.

Struggling with her cargo, she hadn't at first noticed there were visitors on hand. She called out, 'Clive, don't just stand there, love! Can't you give me a hand?' Then she stopped, realising Dr Lowery was not alone.

'Buying up the town again?' he said quite unconcernedly. 'You're just in time to meet our valuable new recruit. Dr Wilde, this is Sharon Price, without whom Beacon House simply wouldn't function. She does our admin and accounts.'

Answering both a proffered hand and a friendly, 'Nice to meet you, welcome aboard!' I reflected that Sharon Price clearly had high intelligence as well as looks above average. She was unlikely to bury herself in this backwater without good reason. Nor was the reason exactly hard to see.

Sad, in a way, that so many susceptible females were ready to surrender to a smile. Whatever my own weakness, at least that wasn't one of them!

While my Grandfather telescoped his long legs into my car, I glanced back once more at the rampling bulk of the old house in the Autumn sun.

★ ★ ★

That evening, the familiar confines of the flat were like a prison. I could neither sit still nor concentrate on polite conversation. We had stopped on the way back for a meal, which my grandfather ate and I didn't.

Luckily a nature programme on the television caught his eye, and I was able to excuse myself for, 'Just a little stroll to clear my head.'

The more I thought about the man with the stutter, the more I believed he was genuine. It was too far-fetched to imagine I was the victim of a hoax. He was genuine, his memory of the accident had haunted him until reluctance to become part of someone else's tragedy was outweighed. So what would he do next with his story? What else but take it to the proper authorities? . . .

'Benita!' a voice called.

Lost in my thoughts, I hadn't noticed a grey car halt beside me. Roger Shepherd was looking out at me with concern.

'I just called at the flat, your grandad said you were out for a walk.'

He had guessed at once where to find me. For only a moment I hesitated before accepting the invitation of the open car door. Indeed, there had been times during today when I longed for his quiet strength.

'Mr Wilde said you've scarcely eaten all day. That just won't do. How about something nice at The Old Farmhouse?'

We managed to park near the small restaurant, just off the shopping centre, which was a favourite haunt of both Roger and his sister, Julie. At one of the tables I spotted at once a familiar figure. It was Julie herself, beaming a welcome.

'You've made it, Benita! Splendid! My Bruce is off at his football training, and I didn't fancy an evening in alone with the ironing!'

It was obviously a well-meaning 'take me out of myself' plot. I submitted at first with resignation, but it was as hard to resist Julie's chatty warmth as it was the delectable Old Farmhouse cooking. There had to come a time when a burden too heavy must be set down, as I had set it down this morning, almost by accident, at Beacon House.

And I talked now about that rather odd establishment. Stimulated by the food and the company, my visit seemed quite entertaining now, from threadbare Smiler snoring among the Superintendent's papers to the monkey-like handyman's exploits at the bathroom window.

Gravity returned with the story of Kylie. Julie asked seriously, 'Do you think staying there will help her?'

'I don't know. Dr Lowery will try his best.'

'You wouldn't really work with a — a charlatan, would you?'

'I'm not sure yet,' I added quite sharply. 'And that's really the wrong word, Julie!'

'I suppose,' Roger's level voice intervened, 'he would be — oh, five-ten, on the stocky side, fair-haired, with a smile he uses like a passport?'

The thumbnail portrait took me completely by surprise. 'You know him?'

'I did, several years ago. We worked at the same hospital. He was involved with a children's clinic there, until he left after some sort of row. Quite predictably, I thought. His methods were considered far-fetched and out of line.'

'Well, things change. People change!' I defended quite sharply again.

The danger of an argument was

averted because Julie had to leave to collect her son from his football. Without her lively presence, a heaviness of quiet seemed to descend.

'Are you serious about working at Beacon House?' Roger asked.

'Well, I'm finished at the surgery. And it's just an assistant's job, all I want at present. You don't think I should?'

'I'd rather you took my advice about a holiday.'

'Oh!' I sighed with impatience. 'What would I do except sit around and think?'

The tables were filling up, with a noisy group right beside us. Soon we got up to leave. I said guiltily, 'I should get back to Grandad, I've left him high and dry. Roger, if you could just drop me back home? Thanks for this evening, I enjoyed it.'

'I'm glad.' Gravely he started the car moving. 'And there's something I have to say to you — though this isn't the time or place, and you should be avoiding big decisions. But it might be better to tell you as you're so worried about the future.'

My heart was beating suddenly faster. It wasn't like him to go into these long preambles.

'I want to ask you if you'll be my wife. I think we could be very happy together. That's what I'm trying to say.'

I gazed ahead at the dark street. I whispered, 'I — I don't know what to say . . . '

'This might make the idea of a vacation easier for you, having something to plan for. We could do some house-hunting. And I was thinking of a wedding early in the New Year? There seems no point in a long engagement . . . ' I couldn't focus on the words. I muttered, 'Roger, I'm sorry! — you must think I'm terribly rude.'

'Of course not. Take your time, think it over.'

He had stopped the car outside The Heights. He smiled just a little wistfully. When he kissed me, for a long moment in that small enclosed world I held fast to him.

★ ★ ★

Grandfather thought I looked better for an evening out. We both retired early. Invariably, early bed and early rising was his motto.

For me, the night meant more long, wakeful hours. So much had happened during that interminable day, but for Terry Stanton, nothing had happened: 'No change', was the answer to my late call to St Anselm's. Finally, I slept when it was almost dawn, to wake suddenly to hazy consciousness of my grandfather clattering in the kitchen.

Also, another sound, the extension phone in my bedroom. Starkly awake now, I struggled up.

Not, as sudden cold dread imagined, the stammering voice of a stranger. Not the hospital, not Roger wanting an answer to the unanswerable.

'So how is Miss Wilde this bright and

shining morn?' an unmistakable voice asked.

Miss Wilde, standing bare-footed and wild-haired, hadn't realised even that the morn was bright or shining. I exclaimed, 'Good grief, not you! At this hour!'

'It's almost a very civilised seven o'clock.' The Superintendent of Beacon House seemed untroubled by that gross lack of respect. 'And you did promise to let me know today about the job.'

'Well — yes, I did,' I conceded.

'Your friend Kylie is right here with me. She wanted you last night. I had to sit up with her . . . didn't I, blossom? So I promised her I'd ring you before breakfast. Can I tell her you're coming?'

'Dr Lowery,' I fairly exploded, 'this is very unfair! Unfair to the child, and very unfair to me!'

'I know. Quite reprehensible. But if it works, why worry?'

I drew a long breath, tempted just to put the phone down. But I didn't put it down. I was thinking of Bradley Wilde's aching concern for me — and it was in my power to send him back happy to Devon.

'Two weeks, no strings attached?' I made sure that was clearly understood. 'All right. You can tell Kylie I'm on my way later today, I've a lot to arrange here first!' So that was that. For better or worse.

There was indeed quite a frightening amount to do before I could leave. Perhaps that was beneficial, giving me no chance to think. First, there was my grandfather to ferry to the station and see off on his way home. I hadn't mentioned last night's proposal of marriage — it was much too soon for that, but certainly he was leaving in a happier frame of mind.

Back in the flat, I wrote my letter to Dr Halliwell — polite, formal, with suitable regrets and vague explanations. I imagined him reading it. Well, he was well rid of me!

It seemed only proper to deliver the

letter to him personally. From habit, I parked in my usual place on the surgery forecourt, yet the familiar premises seemed already like another world.

'Ah, Dr Wilde!' Nancy Shore spotted me from her reception hatch, and informed me that Dr Halliwell was out.

There were still a few patients waiting, with morning surgery running late. As I watched, someone came out of Roger's room and the signal buzzer sounded. Miss Shore got as far as calling, 'Mrs — ' when I intervened.

'Hold it just a moment, please! I won't delay him long.'

Roger Shepherd, busy making a note at his desk, turned towards the door for the next patient, and exclaimed in surprise at seeing me instead.

'I know you're busy, Roger, and Nancy is having kittens out there, but I had to see you. About last night . . . ' This was so hard to say, with his steady eyes on mine. 'I'm not quite ready to give you an answer. I hope you'll understand. And meantime, I'm starting work at Beacon House.'

He leant back in his chair. 'I see.'

I rushed on, 'It's just on a trial basis — probably a couple of weeks will be more than enough! I'm leaving today, later this afternoon.'

He had warned me not to rush into anything. He had advised a quiet reviving vacation rather than a demanding new job. He had asked me to marry him. If I had tried very hard, I could scarcely have behaved in a more unresponsive way.

'I'm sorry,' I said shakily. 'It all happened rather quickly. And I do think the change might help me.'

'Perhaps it will. I hope it does.'

If his quiet response wasn't enthusiastic, neither was it angry or aggrieved. But I still went on making excuses he hadn't asked for. I promised, 'I'll ring you, I'll keep in touch.'

'Please do. I hope it all goes well for you.'

Patients were waiting for him. I felt

like an intruder in a world no longer mine. In another moment I would break down completely.

With tears brimming in my eyes, I turned and walked out.

3

The autumn afternoon had given way to a chill, misty evening when I drove past the lights of Cresswell village. The journey had seemed unending, with traffic snarl-ups reducing speed to a crawl.

Before leaving I had stopped at Wendy Stanton's home but the doorbell rang unanswered. Probably she was at St Anselm's. All I could do was slip a note through her door giving my new address.

Now, I had finally arrived within yards of Beacon House, wearied by my anxious thoughts and the tedious drive. If I hadn't given Dr Lowery my promise, or he hadn't pressurised it from me, very gladly I would have turned tail and headed back home.

Dragging the largest suitcase from the car, I rang the doorbell and waited.

In the chilly porch, various begrimed trainers and boots, a football and a broken skateboard, waited too.

'Come on in there,' I muttered aloud, and jabbed the bell again. This time the door opened a dubious few inches. I glimpsed a blue overall, and a particularly frizzy hairdo through which peered questioning eyes.

'Oh, good evening. Benita Wilde,' I announced myself briskly. 'I've been rather delayed! There's more luggage, but if you'll just show me my room first — '

I heard then light footsteps running downstairs and a new voice joining in. 'I'm so sorry, Benita! I was fixing your room myself, I didn't hear you arrive. Angela, this is Dr Lowery's new assistant, and I've given her the room next to mine. Shall we get her things upstairs first of all?'

Sharon Price, warmly apologetic and friendly, soon had matters organised. We humped my belongings up numerous stairs and along a dim ramble of landing at the rear of the house.

'Sorry it isn't nicer,' she went on apologising. 'There's a bigger room empty, but this gets more sun. If you need anything I'm just along the landing, we're neighbours. Oh, I'll get Barney to fix that squeaky door for you tomorrow . . . Come on, a nice hot cuppa in the staff room before you unpack!'

Again, I followed obediently on. Though the 'staff room' down the landing didn't equal the comforts of home, it did run to a TV, assorted armchairs, a kettle, a toaster, and other similar items.

With the curtains drawn against the darkness, the kettle boiling and the tempting aroma of toast, an unexpectedly strong ache of homesickness was still more eased. Was it, indeed, just my familiar surroundings I was pining for? Far more, I was already missing the nearness of Roger . . . .

'Have you known Clive long?' I asked, knowing this would be an

61

agreeable question.

'Three years. Before Beacon House, he was tied up with a children's hospital in the Midlands. I was in the admin office. Well, I packed up and came here to organise his paperwork, he's hopeless at that. But he's wonderful — with the children.' The last words were added patently out of propriety.

It was easy to please her still more. 'It's a small world, you know! Several years ago my — my boyfriend knew him. Roger was telling me, he remembers him quite well.'

Carefully I didn't quote Roger's opinion of his erstwhile colleague. But Sharon was interested and delighted, asking questions about Roger, eager for details.

'He sounds really nice,' she summed up. 'I'm pleased for you, Benita! I'm sure you make a very nice couple. Come on, tell me some more and let's have another cup and put our feet up!'

But in the midst of more pleasant chat, the door was pushed open.

'Sorry, girls! Am I allowed in, or is this strictly a hen party?'

I looked round at Clive Lowery. Not only had I followed the hint to 'put my feet up' but had kicked off my shoes as well to toast my toes by the fire.

He greeted me, unsurprised, 'Welcome, stranger!'

I answered, 'Er, good evening,' with rather absurd formality.

'Mm. Toast. Mind if I wade in? Any more tea going?' As Sharon hastened to make more, he stretched luxuriously. In some fascination I watched him feed buttery wedges of toast to an attendant Smiler who had followed him in, which were bolted with loud, moist chomping. But it wasn't long before a head appeared round the door, reporting, 'Room Two won't go to sleep,' and 'Frankie Briggs feels sick again.'

Resignedly he stood up, presenting his last piece of toast to Smiler. I volunteered, 'Shall I?'

'Certainly not. Have a good night's rest before you get involved. See you in the morning. Six forty-five sharp, all right?'

Although the man was impossibly self-opinionated and too aware of his own brand of charm, there was genuine kindness and warmth in that dazzling smile. I said in subdued fashion. 'Thank you, Dr Lowery. I hope I won't let you down.'

'You won't! And — the name is Clive.'

When the buzz of my alarm clock jolted me from sleep, I was amazed to find already a grey and misty morning, and even more to blink out at an unfamiliar small room with obnoxious wallpaper.

If last night's homesickness still lingered, I found at once there would be little time to indulge it. Plunged into my first day at Beacon House, the immediate task was 'getting to know the kids'.

Before everyone was ready, the breakfast bell clanged, combining with an aroma of singed toast. There was a stampede to the dining-room. Carried along with it, I found myself expected to preside over a table, where a cluster of suspicious eyes watched my every move. It was Kylie — a disappointingly uncooperative Kylie, not seeming at all glad to see me, who managed to swamp the table with an ocean of milk and cornflakes.

In the midst of this, a tow-haired, pasty-faced boy with oversize glasses kept tugging my sleeve and announcing ominously, 'I feel sick, Miss. Ever so sick, Miss.'

'Take no notice,' the frizzy-haired Angela, clattering by with a trolley, advised me. 'That's Frankie Briggs. Always says he's sick. Never is, though.'

I supposed the boy's nausea was his plea for attention, as dispensing meals around was Kylie's. I told him briskly, 'Nonsense, Frankie, you'll be fine. Eat your breakfast and forget about it!'

I soon had cause to regret it. Angela sympathised, 'Usually he never is . . . '

After breakfast, I supervised the

children in the classroom until their teacher, Mrs Peake, arrived to take charge.

Was it really only ten o'clock? Nor was there any let-up in the day. Dr Lowery beckoned me to sit-in in his office, where he was just starting a first session with Kylie Chambers. This, indeed, was what Beacon House was all about and it was absorbingly interesting. Watching and listening, I realised the warmth and compassion, as well as the skill, in his efforts to reach the hostile child.

Afterwards, when Kylie had returned to Mrs Peake, he spread before me the crude drawings he had coaxed from her.

'What do you notice, Benita?'

'Well. They're more like a five-year-old's work?'

'True. Kylie is well behind her age group. But look more closely. They're all on the same theme, a house. Windows, roof, et cetera. Right, a house stands for home. On this one, some

66

little clouds, birds flying. But what are we missing?'

I shook my head, and then hazarded, 'The sun in the sky?'

'Well done! Any young child will produce a similar drawing with a nice, round, golden sun in the top corner. Once it might be omitted, not five times. No, for Kylie 'home' doesn't tie up with warmth and comfortable security you see?' Mumbling a dubious 'Um!' I just hoped he would succeed.

The day was flying past. But with some time now to spare, seeking sympathetic company, I found my way to Sharon's office. It was disappointing to see my new friend wasn't alone. Clive was utilising the lunch break to sit on the edge of her desk and sign a batch of letters.

'Sorry!' I apologised.

'No, stay, we're nearly through. Sit down a minute,' she invited.

I had scarcely occupied the one available chair when the phone rang, and she answered it smartly, 'Beacon

House! Oh yes, she's right here, hold on! Benita, for you, shall I transfer it somewhere?'

'Oh no, don't bother.' I took the phone from her. Roger or my grandfather would call my mobile during a working day. It could be Wendy with news from St Anselm's?

'Are you there, D-doctor Wilde? Have you thought about what I said last time? What are you going to d-do about it?'

That unmistakable voice! Soft and struggling — and threatening! My answer came sharp with shock. 'What are *you* going to do? Are you going to the police or aren't you?'

'Shall I do that? It won't be p-pretty, one of your honoured profession publicly disgraced ... and you've a family, maybe a boyfriend? Do you want them sitting in a court-room watching you?'

The words were chilling. Always I had half-suspected my own guilt on that fateful night in the rain and darkness, my mind distracted, my body dulled with weariness. Whether Terry Stanton cruelly died or lingered on, the lives of his family were irreparably shattered.

I said shakily, 'Listen, we can't go on like this, it's ridiculous. We need to meet and talk it over properly! Tell me who you are, where you are.'

He didn't tell me. My words served to end the call abruptly. 'I'm somewhere in London, Doctor, and it's a big place. I have to go now, but you c-carry on thinking. You've a lot to lose, haven't you? I'll be in t-touch.'

The line was dead. I returned the phone to Sharon, with my racing heartbeats seeming to fill the room — and aware now of the startled audience who couldn't avoid hearing my end of the conversation.

'Er — trouble?' Sharon asked awkwardly.

'Not really!' Somehow I forced a laugh. 'Someone I know having a spot of bother, probably nothing to worry about. Clive, what's next on my timetable?'

Next, it seemed, was supervising out on the sunny playing-field. I was glad to escape into the fresh air. Half-bare trees pleasantly dappled a stretch of grass which the glum Dan Barnaby had cut this morning with a foul-smelling and explosive mower.

I watched unseeing the flying legs and bobbing hair of the children I was meant to be overseeing, my thoughts in another world . . . a stormy night, a hospital bed surrounded by equipment, a young pregnant girl weeping and weeping . . . And my tormentor on the telephone, that frightening disembodied voice. And now as well, whatever Clive and Sharon had made of my lame explanations?

'Miss!' A hand was tugging my sleeve, and I turned impatiently to Frankie Briggs. He had a new line. 'Miss, aren't you going to stop them, Miss?'

I came suddenly out of my nightmare

haze, to realise a mortal combat was going on only yards away. I hadn't even seen the trouble start, and severe-faced Nurse Potter was well out of reach across the field.

One of the combatants had to be Kylie. Two or three more were involved, a bigger girl with long red hair, and one of the Welles boys, and even as I looked at them, others were joining in the fray.

'All of you, stop that at once! Kylie, you hear me?' I picked on the only one whose name I really knew. But Kylie eluded my grasp like an eel and fled off the grassy field, on to the concreted path. And as she looked back to see if I were giving chase, she tripped and fell heavily, flat on her face.

The red-haired girl stood still and quiet now. The others gathered round in awe, or in curiosity to see the extent of the blood. Kylie was whimpering, with both hands clasped to her face. A crimson stream ran through her fingers.

'It's all right, everyone,' I tried to assure the audience. 'She'll be fine, just carry on with the game.'

'She started it,' the red-haired girl mumbled. 'She called me awful names. I never touched her.'

'We'll sort all that out later! Kylie, let's get you inside.' I saw that the blood came from a split lip and at least one damaged tooth, and by now Kylie was screaming with fright and pain. Other helpers were hurrying across, summoned by the commotion, and the first of them was Dr Lowery.

He lifted the child as though handling a docile infant instead of a half-hysterical eight-year-old, cradling her in his arms. Leaving the other helpers with the group on the field, he turned straight back to the house.

I followed on. In the sick-room, where a couple of days ago I had so successfully managed the rebellious little girl, I stood now watching in remorse and shame.

'No bones broken, no other damage, just that poor mouth. Don't worry, sweetheart,' Clive was soothing her, cleansing the blood and tears gently from her face. 'Now listen, I've a friend in Brighton who's a dentist. No, don't panic, a special dentist who never hurts people. You rest here while I ring him.'

He covered the miserable figure huddled on the bed. At the door he asked me, low voiced, 'So what happened?'

'They were fighting, but I don't really know how it started.'

'Who was fighting?'

'I — I'm not really sure.'

Momentarily I met vivid blue eyes that weren't smiling this time. The brightness in them was anger.

Soon after, Kylie made a dramatic departure. Clutching a luridly-crimsoned towel to her face, she plainly enjoyed the general interest, and the rumours that she had a broken nose/jaw/neck, or had lost all her teeth.

In the back of Clive's somewhat tatty estate-car I made her as comfortable as possible beside me. Of course, I had offered to run her into Brighton myself, but the offer was flatly declined.

The dental surgery was the ground floor of a tall old house, with a tax consultant and other offices on the upper floors. By now, Kylie was utterly subdued. She clung to me tightly in the clinical smelling hallway.

'Hi, Pauline!' Dr Lowery hailed the girl at the reception desk. 'This is Kylie Chambers, the young lady who had the argument with the concrete path.'

'Oh yes, you gave us the details. Mr Compton can see her now. You'll come back for her in about half an hour?'

'No, I'll wait with her,' I volunteered at once.

'Don't, they know what they're doing,' Clive whispered. He bent to coax Kylie, 'Go with nurse, poppet, and if Mr Compton hurts you a teeny bit, tomorrow you shall choose the nicest party frock in the shops. All right?'

Kylie considered. She lisped, 'And thilver thandalth?' 'Tholid thilver,' he agreed.

It was possibly true that Kylie would

be better in the hands of experienced strangers. But I deserted her with reluctance. A moment later, I started quite violently as a warm, consoling arm went round my shoulders.

'Cheer up. How about some tea to calm our shattered nerves?'

He pointed out a small café just across the road. The place was half empty. Two steaming mugs of tea and two wedges of strawberry cream gateau arrived promptly.

'All right, now tell me all about it.' Across the narrow table those disconcerting eyes of his were looking straight into my face. 'Tell me what's troubling you so much.'

A while back, straight after that telephone nightmare in Sharon's office, I might have confided in him, or in anyone. But the moment was long past. The voice of the stammering man was locked away fast in my anxious mind.

'There's nothing to tell. Nothing that concerns you or the clinic!' I blurted out.

'Fair enough. Sorry I spoke!' He seemed unperturbed by that very blunt response. 'If you're really not going to eat that cake? — '

He started serenely on the second portion. But I was aware of that laser-gaze still on my face. I was stung at last to inquire, 'Do you want me to draw some revealing scenes from my past on the back of the menu, Dr Lowery?'

He laughed and said, 'Don't tempt me.' Then he pushed his chair back from the table. 'What an idiot I am! Tomorrow I'm seeing a builder here about an estimate for repairs, so why don't I call there now and save time in the morning? I can get the bus afterwards, if you'll drive Kylie back when she's ready.'

Typical, you might say. He was adept at analysing other people's behaviour, but when it came to disorganised minds, surely his was the most haphazard of all! I agreed, 'Of course I'll take Kylie back.'

'Right.' He tossed his car keys on the table. 'The reverse gear sticks a bit, you just have to let it know who's boss. I can rely on you to look after the kid this time?'

I flared, 'You can!' I knew an annoyed flush rose in my face.

But a new thought followed, born of this uncomfortable scene. I did need some support about the trouble over-hanging me, and it was unthinkable to worry my grandfather. But maybe now Roger really should be told?

And it would be far easier to write to him, easier to put it on paper than to say it, especially in a hasty call when he was busy. A letter, he could digest slowly.

In my bag was a memo pad and a pen. Oblivious to the surrounding sounds of the café, I began scribbling.

It was someone bumping my chair that alerted me to check my watch. I couldn't believe so much time had passed! But maybe Kylie still wasn't ready, so I could finish the letter in the waiting-room. I grabbed up my things and once outside threaded my way through a stream of traffic. I ran the last few yards to the surgery.

The door burst open just as I arrived. I met someone else also running.

'Have you seen her? Is she along the road? Where were you?' Mr Compton's receptionist demanded.

'Sorry, I was a bit delayed. What happened?'

'What happened? I put that child in the back waiting-room while I was tied up and she's vanished through the window, that's what!'

It took a moment for the full horror of it to come to me. The vulnerable little girl lost and alone, the busy town, bewildering crowds, streaming traffic.

'Yes, she's out there somewhere!' Pauline waved an arm at the street. 'And I hope you've a good idea where to look, because I'm not taking the responsibility. I'll ring the police right away and now you've managed to get here, you can deal with it!'

'Small for her age, pale, very thin . . . dark hair . . . she's wearing a red anorak.' My voice faltered over the description of Kylie. So clearly I could picture her. And whatever might happen would be my fault, inexcusably mine!

There was quite an audience. Pauline had duly summoned the local police, whose car was parked conspicuously outside while two officers sorted out details.

At the height of it all, the front door opened. A voice exclaimed, 'Holy Moses, what's all the excitement?'

I fled to that voice. At this moment I knew only huge relief, because Clive Lowery had an uncanny way of making disasters less disastrous. I didn't even flinch at his greeting, 'Not still waiting around here, Benita?'

'I'm here, but Kylie isn't! She ran away! Out through a window!'

The break in my voice really was enough, without more explanations. But I had to confess my gross betrayal of his trust. 'It was my fault. I was late collecting her.'

He didn't turn on me in anger. He nodded, and then wasted no more time on me.

He turned to the receptionist. 'Pauline, my love, you did thoroughly search the house? You see, Kylie is a dab hand at staging dramatic sieges to get attention. One reason her last school parted company with her. Benita, remember our famous bathroom siege?'

I had forgotten it, and remembering, my heart leapt with sudden hope; even though Pauline scoffed, 'I did search, I'm not a fool. There was an open window!'

'Right. But before we take Brighton apart, let's take this building apart.'

He didn't need to do much taking apart. The door of a small cloakroom along the hall revealed, at first, only cream-tiled emptiness — 'I looked in there!' Pauline said triumphantly — but there was also a cupboard, its door slightly open. Within were various supplies, including fresh laundry. Also, an alien patch of red, the scarlet anorak of a dark-haired child asleep in a nest of towels.

As he stooped to coax Kylie awake, her eyes opened like dark wells in her pale face. Their first instinctive fright faded as she recognised him. Already, something in that warm bright smile was banishing some of the menacing spectres from her world.

'No-one came for me,' she accused drowsily. 'I waited and waited.'

'Wasn't that bad of us? But we're here now and everything's fine.'

She was wobbly on her feet, her face bruised and swollen. He lifted her, and she clung round his neck quite contentedly.

I wasn't sure how the whole drama, a moment ago so tense and urgent, just melted away.

Back in Clive's car, dimly aware of the early evening chill, I wrapped Kylie in a blanket. Closing shops and homebound crowds glided past the smeary windows. Kylie sleepily poked him in the back to ask, 'You promised if the dentist man hurt me I'd have a new party dress, didn't you?'

'Did I promise a foolish thing like that? All right, we'll see tomorrow.'

She smiled as far as her damaged mouth allowed. She even remembered to say 'Thank you!'

They were words I echoed, when the warmth and motion of the car had lulled Kylie again to sleep. I said them with tremulous sincerity.

'It was awful! Just awful! If you hadn't called back when you did . . . '

'Did you think I'd go home without seeing George about Kylie? No, there's just one thing bothers me.' In a shaft of light on his face, I saw a rare and ageing frown. 'Just now we need this sort of publicity like we need a hole in the head. If it reaches the ears of my arch enemy Councillor Mrs Fenella Lovelace — '

'The one who wants to close the clinic down?'

'Indeed. Can you imagine the ball she'll have with a story like this?'

There wasn't a word I could say. As he turned the car along the quiet road for Cresswell village, the headlights picking out the lanky ghosts of trees, he was still frowning. And I saw then, quite plainly, what I had to do.

That same evening I did it. With the frenetic bedtime procedures finally over, the big old house dimly lit and more or less quiet, it was past ten o'clock when I tapped on the Superintendent's office door. The light beneath it betrayed his presence. With a snoring Smiler and a bag of marshmallows for company, he was entering up case-notes. I recalled how early this morning his working day had begun.

For the first time, in the harsh light from the desk-lamp, I noticed silvergrey sprinkling his fair hair. As well, there was tiredness in the lines etched in his broad, freckled forehead.

'Sorry to disturb you, Dr Lowery.' I used a deliberate formality that maybe would ease this painful moment. 'It's just, I've this letter for you.'

'A letter?' He took the envelope, and grimaced. 'Oh no! Is it what I think it is?'

'My resignation.' In fact, the second such letter I had penned in a short space of time, and this one had been even harder to write than Dr Halliwell's. 'I'm sorry things didn't work out. I've really enjoyed working here . . . '

'Wait a moment!' he broke in as I was already retreating to the door. 'I thought you gave me a definite commitment of two weeks minimum?'

'Well, yes. But after today . . . ' I spread my hands expressively.

'I know, today was pretty grim. But that's no excuse to renege on our agreement. I can't spare you, and that's final!'

He underlined it by tossing my envelope unopened into the waste bin.

I blinked. It had been in my mind tonight just to drive away, back to the world I had tried to leave behind. I sat down unwillingly.

'Look, it's been a rough day. You're tired and upset. Why not give yourself a chance to get re-orientated?'

'You don't seem to realise. If Kylie had been lost — run over, anything, it would have been my fault. How can I forget that?'

'You can't,' he said simply. 'But in future you'll be wiser, and meantime she's safe in bed dreaming up new ways to scare the daylights out of us tomorrow. That's why I can't let you give up for one mistake. I know you've already abandoned one vocation . . . Doctor . . . ?'

The last word, softly spoken but deliberate, disturbed an unhealed wound. I flinched almost as though I had been struck.

'Yes, I know,' he said gently, as if I had spoken. 'Benita, tell me, couldn't your family or friends talk you out of that? Not even one special friend?'

I muttered, 'You mean Roger Shepherd?' Sharon would have told him about

Roger, that we 'made a nice couple': between them there would be no secrets. 'I talked to Roger. But I did what I had to do.'

He didn't press the point, just leaning towards me in the circle of lamplight, his eyes looking into mine. I heard myself say, half unwillingly and half in longing, 'If you'll give me another chance, I think I've learned quite a lot today . . . '

For answer, he retrieved my letter and held it out to me, 'Here! Put it on ice for the rest of your two weeks.' He didn't just push the envelope into my hand, he held on to my hand too. I was intensely aware of the warmth of his touch, of our nearness in the lamplit room.

It was then, scarcely hearing a soft tap on the door, that I started quite violently as another voice intervened, and I tore my hand free as though it had touched red-hot coals.

'Oh, this is where you're hiding, Benita,' the voice said. It was Sharon's, she of all people. I knew sudden colour was flooding my face, even though my presence here had been purely business. Or at first purely business . . .

Whether or not she had perceived any unusual level of emotion charging the atmosphere, Clive's secretary looked, I thought, decidedly startled.

'Not case-notes, on your first day, at this hour? Clive, what sort of a slave-driver are you?' she asked with a laugh that didn't deceive me.

'The very worst sort,' he answered her. As I stood up to leave, he called me back. 'Oh, one more thing! To recoup from today, take a free weekend. Try some sea air! Monday morning, back for duty bright and early because I've a special job for you.

'You've seen Sharon's notice on the board about our Visitors Day, marking our first year of existence? It could also be our last year, so I'm inviting various official personages along, the ones controlling our purse-strings, to demonstrate our success. The high spot will be an entertainment staged by the children, showing how co-operative they've become.'

'Ye-es,' I agreed dubiously. 'But which is my 'special job'?'

'You can organise the entertainment. I haven't had a chance to bother with the details, and time is running out. Get the kids singing songs or reciting verses — lay on some fancy costumes. Use some imagination!'

For a moment, I just gazed at him. Anxious as I was to assist the work of Beacon House, this looked more a Herculean labour than a special job. He was prompting serenely, 'Any probs?'

'Well, a few! I don't even know the children yet, and this is right outside all my experience!'

'Then it's a perfect chance to broaden your experience, isn't it?'

I drew a deep breath as I turned away. Perhaps I should have made him accept my resignation after all.

4

My free weekend began early on Saturday with two calls on my mobile. My grandfather wanted to know how I was getting on; just a brief chat, and he didn't sound quite his usual self. The second call I missed, and Roger left an equally brief message. He was coming down to see me tomorrow.

'Tomorrow,' I made sure to tell Sharon. 'Sometime before lunch.'

'Oh, that's super, Benita!' I understood her quick enthusiasm. 'I'm looking forward to meeting him.'

I was less sure the visit would be 'super'. Of course I had missed Roger, it would be wonderful to see him. But there had been no time yet to consider his marriage proposal.

As well as those calls, a London-postmarked letter arrived for me, and I read it in the staff-room during a leisurely 'off duty' breakfast in lieu of the scrimmage below. Wendy Stanton wrote, in her schoolgirl hand, that she was feeling poorly and tired.

Perhaps Wendy wasn't the only one near collapse. After yesterday's dramas, followed by a night of broken sleep, I felt utterly tired, grateful to be off duty.

But downstairs, a small figure in a red anorak (I had dreamed about that red anorak!) was waiting to ambush me.

'You ready to go, Miss? To Brighton, where all the big shops are?'

'Kylie, I'm sorry, I'm not on duty today.'

Kylie disagreed. 'Dr Lowery said you was going there, so you'd take me to get my new party dress.' She extended a hand clenched upon some money. 'And he said take Frankie with us, too, 'cos it'll do him good!'

I drew a long breath. Certainly I would be happy to take Kylie shopping, but not today.

But seeing Kylie's still bruised face falling, remembering all her woes of yesterday so largely my fault, I knew I owed the child more than a small slice of my leisure day. I agreed with forced enthusiasm.

A hovering Franklyn Briggs, thin and whey-faced in a parka that reached his knees, was ready. After reporting that I was taking the children out, I glanced at him again and decided to leave my car where it was. On balance, I would rather have him bus-sick than car-sick. In the village we found a bus just ready to start, and it was soon swaying along a sunny road edged by colourful autumn trees.

Once in the big, busy town I made sure to hold Frankie's hand firmly on one side and Kylie's on the other. Kylie was bent on visiting every likely and unlikely shop.

But her final choice, a shell-pink number with a sparkle of sequins, utterly transformed the waif-like child. When the outfit was completed by sling-back shoes with prominent silver buckles, she was even moved to confide out of the blue, 'My mummy had a pink dress. Not like this, but pink.'

I forgot even my growing concern about an increasingly bored Frankie. I knew this was Kylie's first mention of the mother who died some years ago. The whereabouts of her father were unknown, accounting for a succession of foster-homes.

In a crowded cafeteria, Kylie loaded a tray blissfully with goodies. Frankie, steered firmly away from cream cakes and trifles, nibbled a wistful sandwich. Afterwards, we turned along the seafront: in today's Indian summer glory, the sea was sparkling and the sun smiled on the white walls and balconies of the big hotels.

To please the children we crossed the pebbly beach to dip our toes in the water, all standing hand-in-hand in the shivery October channel. Frankie amazed me by identifying a tray of seaweed as 'bladderwrack' and a couple of shells as 'just limpets'. Afterwards, there had to be hot drinks in another café.

Kylie slept during the ride back, pillowed against me, her small sharp features angelic in repose. Frankie sat reverently turning the pages of a new book 'A Guide to Seashore Life,' which I had bought him. Back in the village, we kicked through carpets of dead leaves to the gate in the tall railings. For once, the lighted windows of the old house looked quite benevolent.

Evidently on the watch for us, Clive was at the door to ask how the day had gone.

Kylie admitted grudgingly. 'It was nice. We bought a pink dress. We had masses to eat.'

'Good! And how about you Frankie old son?'

The boy nodded in his awkward way.

As the children vanished upstairs I reported, 'Kylie spoke about her mother, and did you know Frankie is really very intelligent under that hangdog look? Can I go through their files to catch up on the background? — '

93

'Miss W, it's Saturday evening. Another day, yes?'

He was following the children upstairs. I was quite disappointed not to discuss the day further.

*   *   *

Sundays, Sharon had told me, meant 'Sunday tasks' for the kids — letters home, tidying lockers, and so on, followed by either brisk walks outdoors or organised hobbies and indoor games as the weather ordained. No-one was left aimlessly unemployed.

On this first Sunday in residence, I rose late to find a slight variation in routine. Making the most of a fine morning, Clive had ordered a blitz on clearing up the gardens. I surveyed from my window quite a cheery pastoral view of assorted children sweeping fallen leaves and trundling squeaky barrow-loads.

Free weekend or not, I would gladly have joined in. But there was, of course,

Roger's visit, which amazingly had been pushed to the back of my mind. However, I had a short time to spare first.

Kylie ran up to me at once, even though it was just to complain. 'Miss, I can't do all this long path on my own!' She indicated Frankie Briggs huddled under a tree. 'He says just looking at a broom makes him feel bad.'

'Maybe it does. Come on, you sweep and I'll shovel, let's race the twins!'

Greg and Josh Welles put on a spurt with their section of path, and soon quite a hectic contest developed. But when Kylie and I were edging ahead, and she was actually pink-cheeked and enthusiastic in the keen air, we were interrupted. Sharon was escorting a visitor across from the house.

'You've chosen a lovely day, Dr Shepherd!' She was chattering in her bubbling way as she walked beside him, her head not reaching his shoulder.

At this moment I was less conscious

of Roger's presence than of a sudden sharp dismay. I had meant to warn Kylie I must soon go out, but I had left it too late — and now I sensed that to the child's hypersensitive mind, instant desertion in favour of this stranger would seem like stark rejection.

It was all too good a guess. Kylie flung down her broom and fled. I could only exclaim, 'Sorry, Roger, be with you in a minute,' and gave chase. It took some while to corner, calm and partially comfort Kylie, and deliver her to the individual care of Annette Graves. Only then could I pause to realise my welcome for Roger must have seemed scarcely overwhelming.

I found him gravely observing his surroundings from a bench under the trees. At this moment Clive was rescuing a very vocal victim from a patch of thistles. Someone else was stuck up a tree, and the Beacon House 'odd job man' (Dan Barnaby of the odd appearance and permanent gloom) was bringing a ladder and predicting inevitable broken necks.

'Roger, so sorry to run out on you,' I apologised. 'You see, that little girl is new here and she's rather special.'

'That's all right.' His voice was too politely quiet. He might as well have said outright that he considered the whole place a shambles.

'Thanks for coming, it's really nice to see you.' I sat down beside him on the bench. 'I meant to write.'

'Don't worry, I can see how busy you are. But I had to see you to deliver some news personally. Not the best of news, I'm afraid.'

Meeting his serious grey-blue eyes behind their gold-rimmed glasses, all my minor irritations vanished. 'Not grandfather?'

I had guessed right. Roger had received an expected phone call from Devonshire. It seemed that for some time Bradley Wilde had suffered potentially serious abdominal symptoms, and now was entering hospital for 'tests and observation'. He had asked Roger to

pass the news on to me personally —
along with many reassuring messages
that I mustn't worry unduly, and
certainly mustn't rush down to see him.

'Of course,' Roger's level voice went
on, 'this could turn out to be
something quite simple. But I do feel it
would be a good idea if you spend
some time in Devon. Go to him, stay
with him, finish with this place as soon
as you can!'

'I do have a commitment here,' I
pointed out. 'And we're doing important work, though it may not seem like
it just now! But of course I'll stay with
Grandad if I'm needed, I'm sure Clive
will give me leave for as long as it
takes . . . '

Roger's straight-featured face could
be chilly and stern. Its sternness now
wasn't diminished by the sight of
Sharon Price, evidently intent on social
niceties, approaching across the grass
with a companion in tow.

'Here we are, Dr Lowery, Dr
Shepherd. But you already know each

other. Clive, do you remember Benita's fiancé now?' She broke off and laughed, actually drawing more attention to her mistake. 'Oops! I should say, almost-fiancé!'

Clive said pleasantly. 'Ah yes, it all comes back to me,' and offered Roger a grimy hand. 'The Mid-Counties Infirmary — when old Hairy Wilkins was there? He got me turfed out.'

Roger coughed discreetly. 'I believe he did.'

'Still,' Clive chatted on, 'maybe it was for the best, eh? But for old Hairy, Beacon House might never have got started. Benita will explain the worth-while progress we're making. Oh, and I must tell you what a good start she's made, I foresee she'll be invaluable in the future!'

'Indeed,' was Roger's unenthusiastic response to that.

He was eyeing a wan-faced Frankie Briggs who had sidled up to tug my sleeve in his usual way. At the same moment a voice called from the house,

'Dr Lowery! — Can you come? Phone! Urgent!'

Clive shouted back. 'On my way!' and took Frankie's hand. 'Sorry, Roger. Look, why not miss our dubious Sunday nosh and take Benita to the Three Doves in the village. Just tell Sylvia that I sent you.'

Oblivious to Roger's expressive dark brows well on the lift, he added something rather puzzling. 'You two need some privacy, don't you?'

But strolling in the sunshine into the village, we talked rather awkwardly about trivial things — the weather, the traffic on the road from London. The Three Doves Inn provided a good home-cooked meal in pleasant surroundings, and the mention of Clive's name ensured prompt and friendly service. Yet surely, surely, there had been so much more between us than this remote, polite small-talk!

Only a couple of days ago, hadn't I caused havoc by neglecting my duties in order to write to him about those frightening calls from the stammering man? Suddenly, now we were together, I was glad that the letter was never sent! Here in his presence, I knew what his commonsense guidance would be, that the phone calls were a prelude to blackmail, that I should take the facts straight to the police. No, if my persecutor wanted money to keep everything hidden away, I would pay! However foolish that might be, I would pay, I would pay!

I jolted back suddenly to the here and now, as Roger passed some papers across the table with the quiet invitation, 'You might like to see these.'

They were duplicated sheets surmounted by the heading Clay & Withers, Estate Agents. Each of them described 'modern executive-type residences', situated a little way out of London, with attractive photographs.

I muttered. 'Oh!'

Roger was smiling at my confusion. 'I know you've not given your answer yet. These are only tentative enquiries. But,

I never let the grass grow under my feet.'

I lifted my eyes to his, kind and steady. It was true, this was a man who knew his own mind. And he intended to marry me. It was as simple as that.

I whispered. 'Roger, I — I just don't know what to say. Oh, you must think I'm a complete fool!'

'Of course not. You've been through a very bad patch. And that's what I want to change. Suppose we just have a look at this house before someone snaps it up? How about tomorrow?'

'Tomorrow?' I echoed uncertainly. And then panic set in, because I was being swept along, I was losing any sort of control. 'I can't just walk out on my work.'

'I understand. On top of leaving the surgery, you're upset about Mr Wilde. But perhaps it would help him more than anything to know your future is settled?' Across the table, his hand reached for mine: slender, steady, quietly comforting. 'Don't worry about the house. I'll fix a viewing appointment anyway, if you can't make it, I'll look for both of us.'

With our meal finished, we strolled back. As always, Roger had little leisure to spare. It was almost time for him to start back to London. But when we reached Beacon House, all the complications of this past hour fled from my mind — for a stranger's car was sitting squarely on the drive, and a very unfortunate scene was in progress.

The car driver, a bulky, self-important lady in a tweedy suit and too much eye-shadow, had the sort of corncrake voice that carried, even when not raised. And it was certainly raised now.

'I'm not prepared to bandy words with you any further Dr Lowery! All the glorified psychobabble I've heard from you doesn't change the basic facts! You can't deny this child Kylie Chambers has been the victim of negligence, gross negligence.'

'Mrs Lovelace! I've already told you . . .'

'Very gross negligence, and I shall

certainly detail the case in my report on Beacon House!'

The scene was imprinted instantly on my mind: goggling, giggling children, a distressed Sharon beside Clive — and Clive's fair, freckled face crimsoned, his eyes blazing blue fire. Perhaps I should have left well alone. Instead, I plunged in.

'Excuse me, Mrs Lovelace! I'm Benita Wilde, I'm new here, and I can tell you that everything that happened to Kylie was my fault, all mine! As for closing this clinic — I've heard that's what you want to do — don't you realise what a crime that would be? I've watched Dr Lowery at work, and if he's given the time he needs — and support, not blind opposition — he'll produce wonderful results with these children and hundreds more like them!

'Oh, I came here unconvinced, and I've made bad mistakes. But if I can help him in the future, I only hope he'll let me stay and work with him for as long as it takes!'

There I stopped short, aware of three watching faces. One was Clive's, still vividly pink but its anger lost in pleased surprise — and I caught his whisper. 'Bless you, Benita!' The second face was Roger's, set and stern. The third belonged to Sharon, so startled and dismayed that I couldn't understand it — until the obvious explanation dawned on me.

From my first arrival, Clive's secretary had extended a ready hand of friendship to his badly-needed new assistant; so it must seem to her a cruel return if she misread my impassioned defence of him to be a declaration of dawning love for Clive the man!

★ ★ ★

From Mrs Peake's chair at Mrs Peake's classroom desk, just vacated, I surveyed rows of faces. Stony faces, suspicious faces, openly bored faces. Really not the most encouraging of audiences.

My 'free weekend' was over. This was

Monday, I was back on duty — and facing the 'special job' Dr Lowery had so nonchalantly landed on me.

'Settle down, everyone,' I requested hopefully. 'Please pay attention!'

'We've done lessons for today,' the tall, belligerent, red-haired girl in the back row pointed out.

'I know, Jackie. This is about our Visitors' Day concert.' I raised my voice to surmount a chorus of yawns and groans. 'Dr Lowery has left it to me, and I'm going to put on such a terrific show that it'll amaze him as well as the visitors. So I need lots of help and enthusiasm from all of you!'

There seemed little abroad at present. I ploughed on doggedly.

'First, we'll have a discussion to sort out ideas. Who can think of something more fun than an ordinary concert? Come on, hands up!'

A whisper reached me.

'Speak up, Kylie! Did you say a pantomime? Now that's really a brain-wave!'

'Mm. I saw one with them people I was living with last Christmas. It was 'Cinderella'. But if we do it I've got to be her, 'cos I thought of it — and wear my new dress for the ballroom bit!'

It took an animated half-hour to complete the cast list, with people who couldn't or wouldn't act assigned as scene-shifters or programme distributors.

In a way, this project was a way to fill my mind, to the exclusion of other worries almost too huge to contemplate. It was also a real challenge. From Clive I was determined to ask no help at all. I did seek the aid of Dan Barnaby, with a request to construct a prince's throne and a mock-up of a kitchen range. He forecast, of course, that no good would come of it.

Clive's secretary made a point of constantly asking, 'Have you heard from your Roger lately?' But she seemed subdued, not quite the bubbling chatterbox who welcomed me on my arrival. For her sake, I endeavoured to keep out of Clive's way. Particularly, to avoid being alone with him.

Well-meaning efforts which collapsed disastrously at the time of the first full-scale panto rehearsal, a few days on. The whole thing was catastrophic.

To start with, the makeshift platform in the big dining-room wasn't spacious enough, and the curtains came adrift. No-one knew their lines. The Fairy Godmother had a streaming cold.

When the whole crowd clattered off into the fresh air before tea, I sat for some moments in a shattered state. Then, wearily, I began clearing up the debris they had left behind. I was just wrestling with the collapsed curtains, on tiptoe on a chair, when a cheery voice asked, 'All systems go, Benita?'

'Do they look like it?' Breathless and irritated, I looked down on Clive's serene head. 'Of course, this was just a first rehearsal, it'll be 'all right on the night' if it's the last thing I do. But I do happen to be a doctor and not an impresario!'

Immediately, I realised what I had said. If ever 'I told you so' was written in maddening fashion on a face, it was there on his. I amended acidly. 'Make that ex-doctor. And while you're standing around asking questions, you could be fixing this curtain!' 'My pleasure, ma'am', he said meekly.

He took my place on the chair. Though lacking the inches of a Roger Shepherd, at full stretch he could reach the elusive hook.

With a crisp 'Thanks!' I continued clearing up. But a sudden gasp made me wheel round, too late to do anything but watch the flimsy chair topple and capsize him backwards. There was an unpleasant thud as his head met the floor.

'Clive! Clive . . . can you hear me?' In an instant I was kneeling beside him. There was something startling in seeing this man, always so vibrantly alive, lying now so quiet.

It was a huge relief that I saw his eyelids flicker. Somehow I was cradling his head, smoothing back his hair. Maybe not very professional treatment, but it seemed to work.

The clear turquoise-blue of his eyes opened disturbingly near to mine. I caught an appealing murmur. 'Did anyone ever tell you, ex-doctor, what a delightful floorside manner you have?'

'No, they didn't. Did they ever tell you that you're worse than all the kids here put together?'

'Please. I'm suffering. I think I've broken my neck. Benita, shouldn't you really give me the kiss of life?'

What he needed most at present, I thought grimly, was to take his impossible sense of humour, along with the colour of those eyes, somewhere far away and lose them! But there was no chance to say so. We were no longer alone — and the sound of Sharon's high heels warned me who had walked in on this interesting scene.

'It's all right,' I tried to explain rather too hastily. 'Just a little accident, we were fixing the curtains.' Why did the plain truth sound so very lame?

'Were you?' Sharon said. Reassured that the victim was merely shaken, she didn't rush to help. Her face expressed the opinion that he had sufficient help already.

Hoisting my drooping patient none too gently now into a chair, I recommended. 'I think you should lie down a while.' Seeing Sharon retreating I called after her. 'Did you want me for something?'

'Just to say I've done a sample programme for you.'

'Good. Thanks!' I felt guiltier still. 'Shall I come and look?'

'Another time. You seem to be rather busy, don't you?'

At least she wasn't leaving us alone again. Angela and another helper were trundling in a trolley to prepare the tables. The clatter of crockery made Clive wince.

'Angela, my little flower,' he appealed, 'could you magic up a cup of tea for me before the onslaught starts? With four sugars, pet.'

As Angela, her unflowerlike face brightening, flew to comply, I abandoned my work until later. I glanced at Clive without sympathy. For a student of human minds, he was displaying a stubborn stupidity when it came to Sharon's.

* * *

I had a couple of cards from my Grandfather, and a few times I rang him. Each time he told me not to worry about him. From Roger, I heard nothing at all.

Meantime, I was immensely busy with the panto — on top of usual duties. And one particular evening I was left in charge of the establishment: Clive was attending a lecture in London being given by an ex-colleague, and Sharon seemed to have engineered a chance to go with him. I watched them set out, Sharon's prettiness enhanced by a very becoming outfit.

Unfortunately, in the rare absence of Dr Lowery, things didn't go smoothly. I began to despair of getting the household to bed before he got back.

At the height of it all, the phone rang. I grabbed an upstairs extension and barked, 'Beacon House!'

A soft, far-away voice asked, 'Is that D-doctor Wilde s-speaking?'

It took me a moment to believe my ears. Several days had passed since the voice of my persecutor turned me ice-cold. I managed to answer at last. 'Yes, I'm Dr Wilde! And I've nothing to say until you tell me who you are!'

'It doesn't matter who I am. It matters what I can do. I've some interesting pictures on my m-mobile phone, Dr Wilde, not good quality on a stormy night, but good enough. Do you want me to take them to the police? When you've illness in your f-family?'

I breathed. 'How did you know that?'

'Never mind how. It won't help a sick

old man to know there's a serious charge hanging over you. You c-could even go to prison, Doctor, you know that?'

'All right,' I jerked out desperately. 'You've got a price, I suppose! How much do you want to keep quiet?'

'I didn't mention money. But if that's how you want to do things.'

'Let's skip the chat, tell me how much!' I was aware now that my name was being shouted urgently up the stairs by Angela. 'Look, I'll pay something reasonable if you'll leave me in peace, but I'm not rich!'

'Would you call five thousand pounds reasonable?'

I stifled an angry refusal. I could hand over that sum — only for how long would it satisfy him? Wasn't this utter foolishness, even to save my grandfather grief and pain?

'I'll pay that! Just tell me where and when.'

'Very wise. Do you know the Old Ship Café in Brighton? In Hill Street?'

'I'll find it. I need time to get hold of the money.'

'I understand that.' He sounded almost soothing. 'Monday, three o'clock. Old notes, please, and no tricks. Leave it at the counter in a sealed packet marked 'For collection', then leave. I'll be watching. And — c-come alone!'

At the same moment, my arm was being urgently tugged. I exploded. 'Angela! That was a very important call!'

'I can't help it, there's this old guy downstairs keeps asking for the Superintendent, or whoever's in charge, and that's you,' the girl said aggrievedly. 'Some name like Bugler — or Burglar. He won't go away!'

I took a long breath, and patted Angela's arm to show I hadn't meant to snap. Could any visitor have chosen a worse time? With my mind miles away, Room Two still very vocal, and the big lounge looking as though a hurricane had hit it?

Downstairs I faced a tall, severe-faced,

dark-overcoated man and offered, 'Good evening, can I help you? Mr — '

'Bergman.' It was a blessing I hadn't addressed him outright as Mr Burglar. 'I particularly wanted to see Dr Lowery.'

'I'm afraid he's not here. He and his secretary went to London.'

'Indeed!' I came to inquire what progress my boy is making.'

Bergman? My dulled brain revolved the name. Bergman? I said awkwardly, 'I'm sorry, which boy would that be? I'm quite new here.'

'Barry Carter is my stepson,' he explained with heavy patience.

'I see! They're all in bed, but I could bring him down to see you — '

'No, I didn't come here to disturb him. Just to find out his progress — if that's not too much to ask.'

'Oh.' I tried to ignore the barbed comment. 'Well, Dr Lowery's weekly reports will be on Barry's file, so let's have a look.'

At the filing cabinet I paused, giving it a hopeless shake. Clive had one key,

Sharon had the other. Lamely I suggested. 'You could ring Dr Lowery tomorrow.'

'I can ring him anytime! As I was in the district, I thought it was a good chance to get a better picture.'

He was turning back to the door, obviously considering his picture was clear enough already. 'One more thing. I've heard a strong rumour this clinic is likely to close down.'

'It's not true! At least, there are people wanting to close us down as a waste of public money — but they won't succeed!'

'Indeed?' Mr Bergman seemed to doubt it. 'I trust I shall be kept informed. It would be highly inconvenient to have Barry home without notice.'

Almost I retorted that Barry was no bundle of laundry to be sent off with a label round his neck. Though I choked back the words, they could hardly have made matters worse. Assuring the visitor that he would indeed be kept informed, with relief I watched him depart.

It was past eleven when Clive and Sharon returned. She didn't look as though she had enjoyed the evening. Instead of a pleasant time together, perhaps he had just expounded his theories on Frankie Briggs' nausea?

'A visitor came to see you. A Mr Bergman,' I told Clive reluctantly.

'Oh lord, not Barry's stepfather. He's a crusty old devil.'

'He had some excuse,' I admitted. 'I couldn't help him, the files were locked, he'd heard we were shutting down. I think he felt we ought to!'

'I'm sure he did. Unfortunately, he's an influential man. I hope you explained our absence convincingly?'

'Not really, I didn't have much chance, and — I did have other things on my mind — '

'Haven't we all?' he cut short that lame-sounding excuse. 'There's such a thing as diplomatic tact, Benita!'

I started upstairs, simmering and unhappy.

5

It was early on Saturday that I rang Roger's home. With a strong sense of being in disfavour with everyone and everything at Beacon House, I found my thoughts had turned to him often; and recalling his visit here, I felt I had treated him badly, too wrapped up in my work to make him welcome.

Julie answered my call, and there was no doubt at all about the warmth of her greeting. 'Hello, there! Lovely to hear from you! Roger's just leaving — I'll catch him!'

It would be nice, I thought suddenly, to have Julie as a sister. It mattered to me, all at once, to have people close to me.

'Benita?' It was Roger's familiar voice. 'How are you? How are things?'

'Fine, thanks.' Not strictly true, but this wasn't the moment for tales of woe.

'I'm so sorry I didn't ring before — we've been rushed off our feet here!'

'Join the club,' he said wryly.

'You too? Then — ' I blurted out on impulse, 'you didn't go to see that house with the gorgeous garden?'

'No. Perhaps it was as well.' His quiet voice was very serious. 'Perhaps it was a little premature, a little unfair to you.'

Once more I felt a pang of guilt. Last Sunday I had really shown as little interest in the house as I had in Roger himself. I asked, 'Is it still for sale?'

'I've no idea. I could ring to inquire. Why, do you want to see it?'

At this moment I wanted simply to escape from all the misunderstandings and misfortunes of Beacon House. And I wanted to please Roger. 'I just thought — it might be nice to look at the place.'

'I'll ring the agents now.' Roger didn't sound amazed or excited, but then, he never did. 'I'll call you back.'

It didn't take him long. In a few minutes he was explaining the property was still available but needed to be viewed at once. That meant this afternoon. 'I can probably make it,' Roger said, 'but I suppose it's difficult for you?'

It was more than difficult. It clashed head-on with a vital Cinderella rehearsal. I said rashly, 'I'll make it! Where shall I meet you?'

We made arrangements. And then immediately I set to work to act on them. I sought out Clive, who had Jackie in the sick-room with her persistent earache, plus a more than usually pallid Frankie whimpering in a corner.

'I'm afraid I have to go out,' I announced flatly. 'I'll be gone all day. Sorry!' I left him frowning, and grumbling that he was already short-staffed to-day.

Soon I was easing my car out on to the road and away through the village. Beautiful as the countryside might be in summer, its present dank state was uninviting. I was glad to be headed back towards London, and towards Roger.

We were meeting at a railway station just south of Croydon. In fact, I was early, and had to wait. But during the vigil the mist began to lift, even a glimmer of sun seeped through, seeming like an omen. At last Roger's car pulled in behind mine, and I locked the Mini and joined him.

He said at once, 'You look tired. You're still not sleeping well, are you?'

'I'm fine,' I tried to say. My voice almost broke. So badly I needed some sympathy and kindness.

'Well, when we've seen the house we'll find somewhere for a meal while we talk about it.'

The place we sought was not far distant. Woodhurst, with good shops and a park and playing fields, boasted a branch line to Redhill, so was in easy reach of London. In a tree-lined road, the house had white walls and leaded windows.

'It's beautiful,' I heard myself exclaim.

As we left the car, for a moment I just stood still, looking across the close-cropped lawn at rose-beds still jewelled with brave colour. 'It's beautiful,' I said again.

The owners, a friendly elderly couple called Harlowe, were sorry to be going, but since their son had married and left, and Mr Harlowe's health would be helped by sea air, this seemed the time for a smaller home on the coast. For more than an hour, they chatted and exhibited their abode from top to bottom.

'Thank you, I'm sure we're both impressed with the house, Mrs Harlowe.' Roger took his leave with his customary grave politeness.

'Well, I do hope you decide 'yes', Dr Shepherd!' She sounded quite wistful, obviously anxious to pass her treasured home into such careful hands.

At Roger's side I walked back to his car. He suggested, 'How about the restaurant we passed near the park?' We drove in silence back through the town. Roger wasnt pressing me for an opinion. He was very kind.

We sat by a window in the pleasant restaurant, looking out over a green field where a few local boys in businesslike sports gear were assembling, with two supervising adults bearing nets of footballs. I watched them with a sudden stab of pain as I remembered the turn-out on the Beacon House field.

'I think I should go back soon,' I muttered. 'I didn't really have leave today. I just took it.'

'In that case,' Roger said gravely, 'perhaps you should go back.'

'Yes, it's unfair to behave like that. And I'm committed to stay next week, especially for the Visitors' Day. But after that — '

'After that?' he prompted.

'Perhaps I should follow your advice, stay in Devon for a while. And Roger, I still think the house is beautiful. Almost as though it's meant for us, the first house we've seen. But maybe it's too much money?'

I looked into his face, quiet and serious as always. He said, 'The money can be managed.' He reached for my hand and held it gently.

'Well, then.' I gave a nervous little laugh, feeling for a moment absurdly shy. 'Look, help me out! Can't you see I don't know what to say?'

'If you're saying 'yes', there's no need to say anything else.'

'That's — that's what you want, isn't it?' I whispered.

'More than anything else. But only if you're quite certain.'

I nodded. Just a simple nod, but it would change my whole life.

I wasn't exactly sure how or why I had stopped trying to swim against the tide, but the sudden peace of surrender engulfed me. The future Roger had planned was the placid shore where this tide would carry me.

★ ★ ★

By the time I arrived back at Beacon House an early dusk had settled down. I could have returned with a ring on my finger: Roger had wanted to look for one, but I insisted on no official announcement yet and no telltale ring. Far better just to leave quietly and unexcitingly in a few days.

'Miss, where did you go all day?' Kylie accused before I was through the door. 'You promised you'd finish off my Cinderella things!'

'Guess what Frankie did, Miss,' Josh hailed me. 'He fell out of the sick-room window!'

Suddenly, frighteningly, all of my own day and its momentous events seemed remote as another planet.

Clive was just coming out of his office. He asked sweetly, 'Had a nice day, Benita?'

'Sorry about running out on you, but I did have some urgent personal business. Can I speak to you a moment, please?'

I followed him back in. Propped casually against the desk, he waited.

'I've something to tell you. Straight after the Visitors' Day, I'll be leaving to stay with my grandfather, probably a few weeks.'

'I hope he's not worse?'

'No. Thank you. But, I feel it's the right thing to do.'

'I see.' Suddenly that blue-and-gold smile of his dazzled me. 'Don't look like a cat caught in the cream jug. We'll just have to scrape along till you come back to us!'

He had turned to the door, because urgent feet were running along the corridor. In a moment a tearful and furious Sharon had burst in — and she was in no way soothed to find the two of us together.

'While you're chatting in here,' she turned on Clive, 'do you know what those — those little monsters of yours have done? My car, just outside there . . . the paint scratched . . . all smothered in mud and tomato ketchup! — '

He repeated rather weakly, 'Tomato ketchup?'

'That's what I said! Do you want me to spell it?'

'It just sounds a rather — unconventional form of attack. Come on, let's calm down, Sharon.' He reached for her arm, but she evaded him quite violently, her eyes blazing. 'You're telling me the kids have been larking with your car?'

'You can call it larking, I call it vandalising! Those mollycoddled hooligans you're giving your life to,' she flared at him, 'the whole crowd need locking up in a reformatory, that's all they're good for!'

I saw him wince, more shocked at those bitter words than the destructive act that had brought Sharon's inner feelings so revealingly to the surface. In her distraught state of mind she had spoken a sacrilege he wouldn't easily forget or forgive.

'Sharon,' I tried to say awkwardly, 'I'm really sorry. If I'd been here all day, they'd have had less chance. But I promise you, Clive and I will find out whoever's responsible!'

It was an ill-chosen way of sympathising. 'Clive and you!' Sharon echoed. 'Oh yes, you professional people stick together when outsiders like me make a fuss over nothing.'

With those bitter words, she walked out. Even now, the look she gave Clive was more imploring than furious: his comforting arms, his warm sympathy, would have made her forget her woes. But he didn't respond, not even looking at her as she walked past him.

It was a moment for straight talking. I had absolutely nothing to lose. I rounded on him, 'You're supposed to be an expert on minds, so can't you see what's really wrong with Sharon? She's a sweet girl, she's head over heels in love with you — and now she's sure I feel the same and I'm trying to steal you away from her!

'Worst of all, Dr Lowery, she thinks you're enjoying it, like you enjoy flirting with any female between eighteen and eighty!'

After that, I followed Sharon's example and walked out, leaving him frowning, flushed, obviously shaken.

★   ★   ★

It wasn't too hard to discover who had damaged Sharon's car. Earlier in the day, Kylie had been spotted around the out-of-bounds kitchen area, doubtless on the track of a ketchup bottle. To clinch matters, a 'showing of hands' which Clive conducted revealed hers as the only ones bearing fresh scars from some sharp destructive tool, as well as red traces under the fingernails.

I was quite bitterly disappointed. Not for a moment had I suspected Kylie of committing the outrage. Even when her defiance dissolved into an angry, unrepentant admission, I could only watch in chill disillusion. A sense of my own guilt at having deserted my post for the day didn't help.

A while later, when Kylie was in bed and had cried herself to sleep, I told

Clive unhappily, 'I still can't believe it. Not Kylie!'

'She had a reason. She said Sharon shouted at her several times lately. Kylie offered to help clean the car and was called 'a little pest' for her trouble. Well, it sounds possible.' He sighed heavily. 'A sorry business. But I'd like you to talk to the kid in the morning.'

'Me?' I had half expected to be told the clinic had no more need of me. 'I'd like to do more than talk! Shall we stop her being in the panto, showing off her new dress?'

'No. It won't help to take away the little she has. Look, I know you felt you were pulling her out of her dark hole, and now she's jumped right in again, and that hurts. But one thing I've learnt, if today is a loser, tomorrow could be a winner. Just keep on trying!'

Kylie was on my mind all night, even displacing Roger, the house with the dream-garden — and the stammering man. In the morning I was astir early. The hot-water system was up to its tricks again. Room 2 was even less amenable then was customary.

Kylie seemed at first no different from usual, just as distrustful and defiant. By instinct I took her out to the garden, where we could be quietly alone, to coax softly, 'Kylie, wouldn't you feel better if you told me all about it? Miss Price was crying last night, did you know that?'

'Serves her right!' Kylie muttered ferociously. 'I hate her! And she hates me!'

'That's not true. She just isn't very happy at present. When people are unhappy and worried, sometimes they seem cross and grouchy — I'm sure I do!'

Kylie squirmed on the bench under the trees. I went on seeking the right words.

'Dr Lowery almost cried too. You don't hate him, do you?'

'N-no. Well, only sometimes.'

'And do you hate me?'

'N-no.' Kylie wriggled still more, her

ubiquitous red anorak a blotch of colour in the subdued autumn garden. Suddenly words poured out. 'Oh, but — yesterday was so horrible — no Cinderella 'cos you were out, and Miss Price wouldn't let me help clean the car — '

All at once, a flood of tears flowed. 'Miss, he — he won't send me away, will he? I won't do anything like it again, not ever!'

I opened my arms to her. The child's lonely bitterness, the destroying ache of rejection, were frightening. It wasn't nearly enough for Kylie to be fed and clothed, to have a warm bed to lie in, a sound roof over her head . . .

She was sobbing aloud now. 'Miss — if ever — if ever you leave here, Miss, can I come and live with you?'

The tightness in my throat made it hard to answer. 'I live in a flat in London. You'd have no friends, nowhere to play. You wouldn't like it.'

'I would! And I'd do all the washing up for you, honest!'

'Come on.' I changed the subject quickly. 'We need more balloons for Cinderella's Ball, I'm just going into the village. How about helping me?'

Her stricken face lit up. She was even moved to offer, though gruffly, 'Shall I bring my thirty pence and get Miss Price one of them Peanut Chewbars?'

As it happened, with the thirty pence much boosted, we chose an attractive box of chocolates. When we returned Sharon wasn't around, so I put the gift away till later and delivered Kylie to the classroom for the Sunday 'letters home' session.

As I passed Clive's door he called to me, 'Come in and tell me about it.'

I sat down by his desk. 'I hope I got through to her. We ended up with lots of tears — and some chocolates for Sharon. Do you know, even though Kylie appears to hate it here, she was shattered to think you might send her away?'

I tried to describe what had passed almost word for word. Finally I had to add, 'And I see now you were right about still letting her play Cinderella.'

'Good. At present her law is 'an eye for an eye', she'd have hit straight back at us — so where would it end? With one hopeless little girl beating her head against the wall again and again. Believe me, the sense of being by yourself in a hostile world is terrible for a young child.'

'Haven't you any family of your own?' I asked impulsively, my face burning a little as his eyes met mine in questioning surprise. 'I wondered, because you've never mentioned anyone at all.'

'I haven't?' He gave one of his careless, eloquent shrugs. 'It's possible I've scores of relatives somewhere. Don't ask where!'

I muttered, 'Oh, dear.' The chill of my own bereaved childhood had been so much warmed by my grandfather's loving care. 'You lost your parents when you were small?'

'They did the losing. If you want the

details, I was abandoned in a big London hospital — newborn, fetchingly wrapped in a blue blanket — in a corridor of the 'Lowery Wing', named after some ancient benefactor. Hence my name, but which joker supplied the 'Clive' I don't know. Oh, you read these things in the papers, and sometimes a parent is traced. Mine weren't.'

He smiled gently at my disquiet.

'Don't upset yourself, or I'll wish I'd never told you. I don't usually discuss it, I hope you'll respect my confidence.'

'Of course. And, I'd like to say — ' I fumbled awkwardly for words. 'After a start like that, it's quite something to reach where you are today. No wonder you can get through to Kylie and Frankie and the others!'

'Oh well, genius will out.' He dismissed the earnest tribute lightly. 'As for our problem kids, didn't I tell you before you've a real gift with them yourself? You just need to learn how to use it best.'

'I'm glad you think so. I feel I'm

almost as big a failure here as I was in London. Clive, there's something I haven't told you. I resigned from Dr Halliwell's practice because I had to, because he told me I was becoming a liability!'

'I guessed as much. Nasty! I've had the same more than once.' He made a wry, sympathising face as he leant towards me. 'But it's not the end of the road. I always see it as their loss, not mine!'

I was dazzled then by that familiar smile, and somehow by the surrender of both my hands to his.

'Benita, all the Halliwells in the world can say what they like, but what you know you can achieve, you can achieve! That's the truth!'

'Perhaps you're right,' I mumbled. The combination of those turquoise-blue eyes and the warm pressure on my hands made cogent thought more than difficult.

From a distance, voices and clump-ing feet indicated that the letter-writing was over. Clive glanced guiltily at his watch.

'I should have been keeping an eye on those letters. Some of them would make your beautiful ebony hair curl. Well, never mind. You're feeling fit, I hope? I've planned a healthy nature trek this afternoon, a mile of mud and nettles to Leggett's Woods. The kids who don't fall foul of prickles will be frightened by spiders, and Frankie Briggs will feel sick all the way. You'll come?'

'It sounds much too good to miss,' I said gravely.

It was an opinion I had cause to question, after lunch. With colds and stomach-aches among the children, we had a turn-out of ten. Continuing staff problems, plus the absence of Sharon (visiting an aunt and uncle at Portsmouth, and I did understand her need to escape after last night's scene), meant that Clive and I set out in charge of five apiece. I had in tow the Welles boys, Frankie, Kylie, and a tall, moody ten-year-old named Mandy Holt.

Very soon I realised Clive's dire prophesies weren't far wrong. The twins rushed about madly like puppies let off a leash. Mandy, who hadn't wanted to come, moved sullenly at the pace of an aged snail, while Kylie was heavy-eyed and morose in the aftermath of all her traumas. Frankie was his usual whimpering, weedy self.

By the time we assembled with Clive's group in a clearing in the woods, I was more than glad to sit down with my ration of broken biscuits and tepid lemonade. Somewhere along the way, clawing twigs had unhooked my carefully coiled hair, so it cascaded past my shoulders; the first time I had appeared thus in public for a long while.

'Sweet maid, your flowing tresses are the hue of a midnight sky,' Clive murmured poetically beside me. 'Your eyes are like jet, your skin is purer than the pearly woodland mists, and do you know you're sitting on a nest of ants?'

Maybe it was as well Sharon had missed this outing.

Clive was demonstrating what fascinating company he could be: laughing, cajoling, he had all the difficult group playing I-Spy, and then answering a nature quiz. I was delighted when Frankie won that hands down.

We arrived back in a keen rising wind that had faces glowing and conjured up longing visions of hot food. Amid a mass discarding of muddy footwear, Clive asked me, 'Would you step into the kitchen, my angel, and charm our Elsie into an early feeding time, before we have a riot on our hands?'

'I'll try,' I agreed. Belatedly, I recalled something I needed to say to him. 'Clive, I meant to say, I'm really sorry, but I have to see someone in Brighton tomorrow. It's very important.'

'Monday? This Monday? Ouch!'

'I know you're short staffed. And I needn't leave till after lunch, but — '

'OK.' He shrugged resignedly.

* ★ ★

Early in the morning I asked Sharon, encountering her upstairs, 'Did you have a nice day with your family?' She muttered, 'Yes, thank you,' and left it at that. Once she would have chattered on volubly.

The morning seemed to last forever, with Mrs Peake frowning over the chief players in the panto being 'borrowed' from class for extra coaching. Lunch was late. When finally I escaped, my nerves already taut, it took an age to park in Brighton, and there was more delay in the bank where I had arranged to collect the money.

Perhaps it was the sight of those banknotes that brought home to me exactly what I was doing. It was a coward's act, meekly to obey a blackmailer's demands! And yet, this wasn't for myself. To protect my grandfather, to prevent any hint of scandal touching Roger, had I really any choice?

141

More and more harrowing this journey became, for I was already late and the Old Ship Café proved hard to locate. A Chinese takeaway, an Indian curry-house — they didn't help: I was starting to breath, my hands were clammy. Not the ice-cream parlour, nor the tearoom with its fussy lace curtains . . .

But there I stopped suddenly short. There was no mistaking the girl sitting near the window, her attractive face in profile. And no mistaking the companion with whom she was sharing a pot of tea, an imperious-faced woman with a blue-grey hairdo and matching eyeshadow.

Sharon Price and Mrs Lovelace! Deep in tea and scones and earnest conversation, Clive's trusted helper and the local councillor who considered Beacon House a good site for redevelopment!

Had Mrs Lovelace arranged the meeting, hoping to persuade inside information out of Sharon? Or was it possible Sharon had jealously, vengefully embarked on a campaign against Clive? For a moment I considered just coolly joining them, to attempt to gauge what was going on. No! Blundering in might do more harm than good.

It was a glimpse of the tearoom clock that jolted me back to my own desperate problem. Twenty-past three, and I hadn't yet found the café! It took more minutes of feverish searching and asking before I located the place.

My heart was pounding as I went in. Behind the counter a woman in a navy tabard presided over a steaming urn. A bored young girl was wiping the tables. No anonymous figure in a hooded coat and big sunglasses, concealing his face with a handkerchief — the sort of set-up I had vaguely imagined.

But of course, he wouldn't linger past the agreed time. I had missed the appointment.

I asked shakily for a coffee. It was unthinkable to risk leaving my package at the counter now. In another five minutes, I was walking quickly back to my car.

The two fresh problems I brought back to Beacon House, missing that so vital appointment, and spotting a strange tea-party, had to be faced somehow. I did my best with them. Since I couldn't contact my persecutor, the only course was to lock the money away in my room and wait.

As for Sharon, I decided it would be unfair to carry sensational tales to Clive before first confronting her myself — which might uncover the truth, because Sharon was a transparent soul.

The arrival of the morning mail the next day chased all else from my mind but one typed envelope holding one sheet of paper. IF YOU WANT TO PROTECT YOUR FAMILY, IT WAS FOOLISH NOT TO SHOW UP ON TIME, DOCTOR. Just those few typewritten words, but there would be more, another note, another phone call, this cruel war of nerves going on and on!

In an impulse of anger and disgust I was tempted simply to ferry that paper straight to the nearest police station. Only, in the same post was a card from my grandfather's hospital bed. 'I haven't been quite so well, Bennie,' he wrote — who so seldom admitted to any illness.

The unanswerable problem nagged at me while I struggled with hectic last-minute preparations for the Visitors' Day — last-minute because of Clive's cheerily haphazard sense of timing. At ten o'clock that evening I was still busy, helping him give a hasty 'face lift' to the main staircase.

So, in old jeans and a baggy sweater, my hair scooped back in a scarf, I was immersed in the job. 'No need for finesse, just paint over the graffiti and parked chewing gum,' Clive had instructed. We were scarcely half-done when I heard vague sounds of arrival below: Angela hissed up at me, 'Someone here to see you!'

The late caller was Roger. He stood

at the foot of the stairs, tall, gravely disapproving, dark-suited, his nose wrinkling slightly at the reek of new paint.

'Well!' I exclaimed. 'You're the last person I expected to see!'

I was too amazed to feel or express any pleasure. Chiefly I felt guilty — because I should have phoned him long before now about the Beechnut Drive house.

But must he stand there like a statue of chilly disapproval? Of course, he would have had a long hard day. It was late, he was tired — and it must be disconcerting to be greeted so casually by a dishevelled paint-spattered fiancée. But couldn't he at least save his annoyance till we were alone?

Apparently not, for he was putting it into biting words. As Clive waved to him from higher up, he asked frostily, 'Dr Lowery, am I right in thinking Benita came here to help with your patients, normal duties and times, not as a round-the-clock factotum?'

Clive rubbed his nose with a sticky yellow thumb. 'Technically, yes. But you try roping in our resident handyman at this hour! And it's an emergency.'

'Yes, an emergency!' I burst in with more warmth than diplomacy. 'Roger, I offered to help, so don't blame Clive!'

'Obviously you can't see when your willing nature is being exploited. It's fortunate I can. Please allow me to settle this and don't interfere.'

'Interfere?' I echoed the abrasive word. 'Look, I live here, I work here, I'm not a child, and if I want to paint ten staircases I needn't ask your permission!'

It was the first time I had ever raised my voice to him. But then, as the absurdity of the scene struck me, I tried to laugh. 'Come on, this is silly! I'm glad you came, I've been wondering how you got on at Clay and Wotsit, the house agent people.'

He said, 'Indeed?' but the lift of his eyebrows said far more. I hadn't wondered enough to pick up a phone.

'Well, at least give me credit for some manners!' I said acidly. 'I do intend to stop work and find you a cup of tea. That's if you'll please stop looking at me as though I'm something the cat dragged in!'

Again, I had raised my voice. It was unthinkable to be squabbling with Roger at all. The real trouble was, of course, he was jealous of my absorption in Beacon House, and in the man who ran it. And I was overstressed and equally angry, because being engaged gave him no right to be so unbearably high-handed!

'Sorry, folks, but could you cool it?' Clive intervened from higher up the stairs. 'If you wake the kids while this paint is wet — '

They were prophetic words. The Welles boys were already on the middle landing, crying in gleeful unison, 'Yippee, paint! — We like painting!' They stormed down with the grace of an elephant stampede.

For an instant, I shut my eyes. I didn't want to know if they were Greg's feet on the wet surfaces, or whether Josh's rush had sent a paint tin rolling in a stream of yellow to the hall below. There was worse to come, for sounds from above indicated that others were about to join in.

Clive made a dive for the landing to bar their way. From somewhere came Frankie's dismal wail, 'Paint always makes me ever so sick.'

Trying to hold a struggling twin in either hand, I had no breath left for Roger. I heard his clear, deliberate voice amid the chaos: 'I'll see you another time, Benita, well away from this madhouse!'

⋆　⋆　⋆

It was past midnight by the time the twins had been scrubbed clean while I dealt with Frankie. Finally, everyone was back in bed and work recommenced on the yellow disaster of a staircase. The last blow came when, due to all the wastage, the repainting had to end two steps short.

I stood beside Clive in the hallway to survey our work, both of us equally shattered. He was still philosophical enough to suggest, 'Could set a new fashion in décor, maybe?'

My lips twitched involuntarily with amusement as I looked at his heated, freckled, canary-smeared face that bore a distinct resemblance to some Indian Chief's warpaint in an old Western movie. I agreed, 'Maybe. Oh, this has been such a day, I don't know whether to laugh or cry.'

'That's easy. Laugh!' he advised.

He followed up the advice in a way that took me utterly off guard. I felt his lips touch my cheek, just a playful, comforting kiss. And then he whispered against my rumpled hair, 'Apologies to Roger' — and the next kiss was full on my lips, warm and lingering.

No-one had ever kissed me like this. Not Roger, not anyone. My heart was racing, my head swimming from tiredness, from shock, from his nearness. 'Good night, Bennie,' I heard him say as the arm around my shoulder slipped away.

Somehow I staggered upstairs. It seemed as though I was living a dream, lost and adrift, utterly bemused. All of today was like a dream, and all a waking nightmare, until those final moments.

It was exhaustion that brought me sleep. I woke unrested but clear-headed. Very early I rang Roger's home: there was no answer, and I didn't try further — for still I felt our difference was largely his fault. It wouldn't harm him to do the ringing and apologising.

It was a relief that Clive said, 'Morning, Benita!' just as usual, as though last night's summit of emotion (due, no doubt to excessive stress) hadn't happened. Mercifully the postman brought me no more typewritten notes, but Clive informed me later of confirmation that two particular individuals would certainly attend tomorrow's Visitors' Day. One, the stern Mr Bergman — and the other, of course, Mrs Fenella Lovelace.

It was early evening when a final dress-rehearsal of Cinderella began. Until now I had picked out a musical background myself on the Beacon House upright, but tonight Clive offered his services, allowing my full attention to the stage.

And it was needed. All along, Mandy had been difficult, wanting to play Cinderella or nothing: tonight she reached the point of hitting Prince Charming — that so deceptively angel-faced Paul — over the head with her magic wand, which he promptly grabbed and snapped in two. Mandy stormed off the stage, the cast took sides, and chaos ensued. In the midst of this, Angela called from the back, 'Miss Wilde! For you!'

There was an envelope in the girl's hand. One glance at it was enough.

'Angela, where did you get this? Who gave it to you?'

'Dunno, Miss. Came in the door, didn't it?'

'But surely you saw who brought it!'

She shook her head, and I forced a nod and smile for her. How could I blame her for missing a man who would have slipped stealthily away? I felt my flesh creep as I realised that, only moments ago, he had been just yards from me.

Suddenly I realised as well that everyone was staring, wondering what was wrong with me. I mumbled an excuse to Clive and followed Angela out. The vital rehearsal would have to wait. In the corridor, I ripped open the envelope.

Ready for new instructions to pay probably double or treble the money, I wasn't ready to find a newspaper cutting, a black headline RECKLESS DRIVER JAILED, and a paragraph below reporting the case of a young victim crippled, a criminally negligent motorist duly punished. Most shocking of all, the driver's name had been blanked out, and my own name written in.

A moment ago I had recoiled at my persecutor's nearness. That was nothing to the revulsion now in holding this paper his sick and grasping mind had contrived. A wave of physical nausea, surpassing any poor Frankie could have suffered, made my blood turn to ice and my head dizzy.

'Will you show me that?' a voice asked beside me.

It was sheer instinct that made me crumple the paper behind my back. I looked at Clive and saw his eyes drained of all their laughter, the stern lines of his face making it a stranger's.

'Show me!' he repeated. 'You're being threatened — blackmailed? Do you think I can allow it to go on under this roof, among the kids who've been entrusted to me?'

'Oh . . . the children! I — I didn't think about that . . . Please,' I appealed painfully, 'I promise I'll deal with it! I know I've been stupid, but I'll put it right this time . . . ' The earnest plea went unheeded. The paper was wrested roughly from my hand.

'Just as I thought,' his unpitying voice said. 'Very well. Please wait for me in my office. I'm abandoning the rehearsal — I need to get the kids sorted out.'

He was quickly back with me, I sat beside his big untidy desk rebelliously, still sick, still angry. Nor did the unsympathising, exhausting inquisition that followed do anything to help. I discovered he had been observant enough, over the past days, to put two and two together: those obviously shattering phone calls I received, plus yesterday's letter and today's message — but chiefly a very revealing page of my unfinished letter to Roger, accidentally dropped in Clive's car during the adventure of Kylie and the dentist. Clive had read it, and kept it.

'You had no right!' I burst out. 'It was personal!'

I might as well have saved my breath. And indeed, I needed it all to answer his onslaught of questions. Somehow the whole sorry story poured out. I was half crying by the end of it.

'Perhaps now you'll believe I was trying to spare my grandad — and Roger — and not just protecting my own skin!' I flung at him. 'I'm sorry I didn't think of any danger to the children, or bad publicity for the clinic, but you might try to understand how awful I've felt, you might have some humanity!'

I started to get up. Though my legs were shaky, my voice suddenly was steady. 'I'll go straight back to London — and tell the police every single thing I've just told you!'

'Hold on. With tomorrow the Open Day? Is it too much to expect,' he suggested unpleasantly, 'that you shelve your sordid private troubles till you've at least tried to complete the job you came here to do?'

I just looked at him. Where was that

winning golden smile now?

'I find I have to go out in the morning.' He tipped his chair back in his familiar maddening fashion. 'A couple of calls — and I'm not sure I'll be back for the visitors. As you're still my assistant, you'll be deputising for me till I can take over. All right?'

I muttered an inadequate, 'Good grief!' When it came to barefaced nerve, Clive Lowery had everyone else beaten hands down. 'A couple of calls' was an absurdly casual excuse for walking out on the day he was most vitally needed!

'Can I also remind you,' he was asking, 'that to-morrow could be a 'shut-up-shop' day if things go wrong? So can you try to make less of an unholy mess of it than you've made of everything else so far? Is that quite clear?'

My voice returned to me, with dignity, with deliberation.

'Quite clear. I'll do my best for the children. And as soon as it's over I'll take myself and my 'sordid troubles' out of your way.'

At the door, I turned to add, '*Permanently* out of your way, Dr Lowery!'

6

I exclaimed in futile anger, 'I don't believe this!' I blinked, hoping the sight might go away. But it didn't.

After breakfast, I had been summoned by a member of the kitchen staff. One of the large rubbish-bins contained, not only the usual waste, but also those pantomime costumes on which I had spent so much time, along with all the ballroom decorations. Everything was torn, dirtied, spoiled.

The girl was saying in awe, 'I did look for the Superintendent to tell him.'

Clive must have made an early start. His car was already absent. I said mechanically, 'Thanks. I'll deal with it.'

In fact, a worse discovery awaited me. When I rounded up the children, they were one short. Mandy Holt was missing, as well as her 'magic coach' bicycle. (She had very reluctantly agreed, a couple of days ago, that her gleaming new machine could be dressed up with tinsel to serve as Cinderella's transport to the ball.)

I was determined not to panic mindful of past experience with Kylie. Tinsel scraps leading out to the lane indicated that Mandy had artfully seized on a moment when the gate was open to sneak off the premises, and had ridden towards the village.

Between breakfast and now she couldn't have gone far. Leaving the senior staff-member, severe Nurse Potter, in charge, I was starting up my car when Jackie ran across, her fiery tail of hair tossing.

'Miss! I know why she spoilt the things and ran away! Her Auntie she lives with, goes raving mad when Mandy isn't top in everything. She told me once. Well, she's only fill-in Fairy Godmother because I had earache, and I'm better now.' She glowered at me. 'Well, if her Auntie's coming today, let Mandy do the part! I don't want to be in the boring old panto anyway!'

From the over-belligerent Jackie, it was consideration undreamed of. I said quietly, 'That's very helpful, Jackie. I shan't forget it.'

If 'Auntie' did arrive today a few words must be said to her. As for 'Cinderella,' it was unlikely to be staged at all. But the only need at present was to bring back the runaway.

I drove into the village, noting more tell-tale tinsel along the way. First I intended asking around if Mandy had been seen. But as it happened I had no need, for the prayer in my heart was answered as soon as I reached the cluster of shops. Leant up against the corner sweetshop was a shiny bicycle, now a little bent and scratched, still trailing a bedraggled glittery festoon.

In the shop, surrounded by sweets, magazines, a few Christmas cards and wrappings blossoming on a stand, Mandy was perched on a chair to have a damaged knee tended by the elderly shop-owner, mild and kindly Mrs

Marshall. Just in time I barred a wild rush to the door, as Mandy screamed at me, 'I'm not going back! I'm NOT!'

'Then she is one of yours, Miss — er — ' Mrs Marshall said. 'She came off her bike with such a bump. I was going to phone you, dear, but she said she didn't live at the Clinic.'

'Well, I don't any more!' Mandy was still fighting my grasp. 'I'm going to my grandma in Australia, see? And don't think I can't do it!'

'I'm so sorry you've been bothered,' I apologised to Mrs Marshall. 'I'll look after her. And I'll send someone down for the bike.'

As I towed my charge to the door, the concerned old lady stuffed a packet of sweets into Mandy's pocket. I was relieved it wasn't thrown straight back.

Outside, the car waited. The worst worry of all was past, but what was to be done now with Mandy, with the ruined show, let alone the unknown hurdles of the Visitors' Day ahead? How would Dr Lowery deal with it all?

Angrily I discarded that thought. Never mind him, who had offloaded all the responsibilities! How would I deal with it myself?

First, I sat in the car with Mandy, earnestly talking to her. Most of all I kept insisting I was deeply grieved that she hadn't understood there were people ready to share her troubles, anxious to help. I was upset too that she hadn't considered the other children who had worked so hard on the show, now in vain.

Mandy was not another Kylie, with fragile emotions ready to break into fiery rage or aching tears. Locked in sullen misery she scarcely spoke the whole way back, when at last I deemed it safe to drive. Only when we were almost there, she muttered, 'My grandma did say I could live with her! She did!'

'Very well. Then suppose I speak to your auntie and ask if maybe they can arrange a sort of trial visit first? But you'd have to earn it, Mandy. Have you really earned it today?'

For the first time, tears welled in the girl's eyes. I looked on it as a victory. Still more, her mumbled words at the sight of watching faces and pointing fingers marking the car's arrival. 'They — they'll all hate me now.'

'They won't. They'll be sorry you were so upset.'

Upstairs, quiet and secluded, I inspected the hurt knee and then settled my patient on a bed under a rug. Then I stood a moment doubtfully by the door.

Mandy said tersely, 'Lock me in, I don't care. My auntie used to.'

'No. I just want you to promise, next time you feel the urge to wander, tell me first. Just tell me!'

I went downstairs, with the idea of assembling all the children. But to my surprise they were waiting for me. An excited buzz of chatter died as I arrived.

I announced as brightly as I could, 'Well, everyone! Mandy will be all right, she's sorry for what she did and hopes you'll forgive her. But I'm afraid we'll have to cancel the show. Maybe we can just make up a concert of the songs we've been practising.'

There was a chorus of dissent. Kylie spoke up clearly above the commotion.

'No, we know a way to do the panto. We've got it all fixed up! Frankie and me done it all, Miss.'

'You and Frankie?' I echoed a little weakly.

Frankie Briggs, whey-faced as ever, nodded so earnestly that his oversize glasses slid still farther down his nose. In fact, it was a simple scheme, to stage 'Cinderella' in everyday attire! Prince Charming would cut a dashing figure in immaculate school uniform, while his page wore jeans and a teeshirt. Frilly nightdresses would double for party gowns.

As for the 'ballroom spectacular', it would be achieved with scattered flowers and leaves from the garden: Frankie's idea, and he had been industriously gathering them. While the fairy coach, that piece de resistance was to be Gary Bailey's skateboard!

The way in which everyone rallied round convinced me that I had, despite everything, made a real impression during my brief time here. And their helpfulness brought a new idea to me.

While they were so co-operative, might it be possible to organise 'guided tours' for the visitors, with each child conducting a guest around and answering questions about the daily life of the Clinic? Risky, of course! But if it succeeded, what could demonstrate more clearly that these young 'unmanageables' were being transformed?

'I'm sure you'll have a smash hit with the panto, everyone!' I told the expectant group. 'Now, will you listen to my idea?'

They listened. Despite a few grumbles they agreed to do their best. If this Visitors' Day turned out a failure, it might be the result of Clive Lowery backing out of it, but in no way would the children or I let it fail for want of trying.

Lunch was very early so that the big dining area could be cleared rapidly of its tables and set up as a theatre (entailing much muttering, puffing and blowing from Dan Barnaby.) From two o'clock the doors would be open.

When the first cars began arriving I scanned them to see if Clive's battered blue estate was among them. It wasn't. As I took one last glance from a landing window, Kylie's dark head bobbed under my arm.

'Not back? Well, that's men all over. Never trust 'em, my mum always said.'

Hastily I diverted her attention to a large and gleaming car just drawing up, its occupant a bulky lady with a blue-ish coiffeur. 'Kylie, that's Mrs Lovelace, a very important visitor. I want you to take special care of her. Will you do that for me?'

'Course,' Kylie agreed conspiratorially. 'I'll give her the works, Miss.'

A gamble, if ever there was one. One more among all today's gambles.

Downstairs, I hoped I looked calmer

than I felt, as I plunged into one of the most difficult afternoons of my life. It was a drawback that I knew by name not one of the guests, excepting Mrs Lovelace and Mr Bergman — whom I would really rather not have known. It would have helped had there been more time to digest Clive's extensive case-notes. Perhaps it would have helped most if I could produce a decent excuse for his absence.

'He must have been delayed. It's most unfortunate!' I kept saying.

By now, two officials from the Health Department had arrived. I brought forward the refreshment interval, risking rebellion in Elsie's kitchen, in hopes Clive would still come, but Clive didn't come. I tried to chat pleasantly and tactfully to everyone — especially Mandy's 'auntie', a languidly attractive lady in a smart ensemble. Neither Kylie nor Frankie had any visitors.

The next stage of the programme had to be started. While the children made ready for their show, I sat at Mrs

Peake's desk to address the guests on the aims and hopes of the clinic, ad-libbing as best I could. After that, there had to be a 'questions' session, and I battled through it somehow.

Sharon Price, who could so much have helped, simply did not appear except for a brief look-in during tea. She said she 'couldn't leave the office.' I was facing this completely alone.

★   ★   ★

At four o'clock, amazingly on schedule, the curtain rose on the high spot of the day. I told the audience, 'This show has been produced entirely by the children, at very short notice.' I sat at the piano in a sudden fever of apprehension.

But from the moment Greg marched on stage as Baron Hard-up, puffing importantly at a chocolate cigar which he almost swallowed, it was clear this would be a comedy hit. Everything that could go wrong went wrong: the various 'props' developed minds of their own, lines were forgotten wholesale and prompted in piercing whispers there were frantic audible arguments off-stage, 'We've done that bit!' — No, we haven't!', 'Paul's jumped right into the next scene!' Yet all the complications only added to the hilarity.

And through it all, Kylie's rendering of the name-part brought flashes of true pathos. Frankie's 'special effects' brought down the house.

I realised suddenly that someone was standing by my piano-stool. Exactly when Clive slipped in, I had been too engrossed to notice.

He gave me a wink and a thumbs-up sign. And well he might, as the audience gave their enthusiastic applause. Now they too had spotted his presence, the adulation was not merely for the children.

'Dr Lowery, that was quite remarkable!' . . . 'We're really impressed!' . . . 'You've certainly worked wonders!' . . . Serenely he accepted all the praise, just a couple of times waving a hand towards me and acknowledging. 'Today was largely due to my very able young assistant here.'

Nice of him! And altogether typical to arrive back just in time to soak up all the praise!

Kylie was being showered with congratulations on her performance. But, looking for Frankie, I felt his familiar tug on my arm. He asked dismally, 'Miss, can I go outside? . . . ' and I made urgent signals to Annette Graves. There was no danger of success going to Frankie's head; it went, like most things straight to his stomach.

It was hard to realise Visitors' Day was over. I had given it all I had to give. Now, suddenly exhausted, I echoed farewells and shook a few hands. The last stragglers were the Health people, busy in discussion with Clive. Well, the future of Beacon House was no longer my concern. While the children swarmed upstairs and the big room was being restored to order, I waited until he was free, and then waylaid him.

He asked brightly, 'How's the great impresario? Ready for a niche on Broadway?'

'I said I'd do my best for today. Now I'll pack up my things — ' My voice was quite steady. 'As I told you, when I reach home I'll contact the police straightaway.'

'Very laudable. But wait just a moment. You've some personal visitors coming — and it looks like they're just arriving.'

Not understanding, I peered through the window into fast-gathering dusk. A familiar car was pulling up. It couldn't be Roger's? . . . and yet there was no mistaking the tall man just getting out. 'I exclaimed, 'Clive, did you tell him what I'm going to do?'

He didn't answer me, already opening the door. But that must be the answer! And Roger, in his concern for me, was here to help me through the ordeal ahead. I should never have doubted him, nor underestimated his loyalty.

But Roger was not alone. He was escorting a young girl with loose, light-coloured hair, obviously in the late stages of pregnancy. Wendy Stanton! And beside Wendy was a stranger, a young man, a little hunched of shoulder, very pale of face.

Somehow, Clive swept us all through to his office. He invited briskly, 'Sit yourselves down, folks! We've some talking to do.

'Roger, will you put Benita in the picture, or — '

'I'll leave it to you,' Roger's level voice said.

I was aware of my racing heartbeats as I gazed from face to face. Neither Wendy nor the stranger had once looked at me while they were being ushered in. I watched Clive take his usual place at the desk, and then the silence broke as he began talking in his facile way.

And the very first fact I learnt was the real reason he had deserted Beacon House today of all days. This morning he had driven to London with the express intention of sorting out my own personal problems! So far, I had totally misjudged him.

His first concern was to take directly to Roger Shepherd the whole dramatic story pressured out of me last night. He considered my future husband needed to know. Deeply shocked, Roger at once laid aside all personal enmities to assist him, even agreeing to follow up a 'hunch' of Clive's about the identity of the blackmailer.

For when wresting the tale from me last night, by bullying me into angry defiance since all gentler attempts had failed, there stirred in Clive's mind suspicions of Wendy Stanton. Not merely due to her readiness to accept 'hand-outs', but because the blackmailer knew my movements, my family affairs, even my grandfather's illness. Logically, the blackmailer must be someone I knew — or, at least, be in that person's confidence.

So, Clive and Roger walked in out of

the blue on Wendy. They found her with a friend, a little older than herself, deceptively pleasant-faced and nervous-mannered. So nervous, indeed, that he spoke with a very noticeable stammer . . .

'Isn't that right, Andrew?' Clive asked him now across the room.

The bent head didn't lift, the stubbornly downcast eyes weren't raised. But the voice that answered turned me suddenly to ice. 'I've n-nothing at all to s-say.'

Nothing to say, because already that voice had said enough, haunting me with its cruel whispers. A voice I would never forget, forever a nightmare in my memory. In the shock of hearing it now, I sat as still and mute as he. But Clive needed no more confirmation, going on quite cheerfully with his story.

In Wendy's home this morning, with the tell-tale stammer I had described ending all doubts, Clive accused the stunned conspirators in a blaze of anger — and grabbed Wendy's phone to ring the police. It was too much for Wendy. She burst into floods of tears, and the whole miserable tale poured from her.

How she and Andrew had been 'almost engaged' before Terry Stanton entered the scene — older, more forceful, to sweep her off her feet and straight to the altar. How, over the past year while Terry worked all hours to improve their home, she began secretly seeing Andrew again. And inevitably came the day when her husband, a man of quick temper, found out. It was after a violent 'eternal triangle' row, one rainy night a few weeks back, that Terry rushed headlong from the house, and blundered unseeingly in front of my wheels.

Andrew Parker was only seconds behind him, implored by Wendy to run after her husband and try to bring him home. From a little distance he watched the helpers attending to the figure on the wet roadway — and indeed, filmed the tragic scene on his photo-phone, but without capturing the actual impact. He saw the ambulance. He saw me, the dazed and distraught driver.

For a while after that night the friends kept apart, aware they had driven Terry to his death, or near death. But the days passed, the shock dulled. Though Terry didn't improve, nor did he die. And, little by little, they began meeting again. They deluded themselves, 'It was far more the motorist's fault than ours, she must have been driving like a lunatic!'

Just at this time I began offering gifts to Wendy, an act they gladly hailed as proof of a guilty conscience. It was just one step more to decide Dr Wilde ought to recompense her victim far more generously. Andrew, outwardly so inoffensive, evolved a cold-blooded scheme to milk me of every possible penny: I deserved to suffer, I deserved to pay! And of course, the payments would be shared, doubtless his share the larger.

In fact, they never really set out to be

criminals, especially Wendy, a grief-stricken teenager, easily persuaded. But she hadn't said 'No', and so now she stood in no less trouble than he. Very grave trouble it could be, Clive had told them this morning. The law did more than frown upon blackmailers.

Had matters been left to Roger, the conspirators would have been handed over at once to justice. Only with reluctance did he delay, on Clive's insistence that this decision must be mine and only mine.

It was a decision I had already made, for my anger had faded along with the agonies of fear and worry. Especially, I couldn't bring more trouble to Wendy. The girl had already suffered enough, and her sufferings were far from over. Only in deep pity, watching Wendy sobbing in a huddle of misery, I told her again and again that all was forgiven.

But other arms were already comforting her. Beside her on the well-worn settee, Clive gathered the weeping girl close like one of his own flock of straying children.

'That's right, let it all out. Just remember, you have a living husband, Wendy, and a living child. They're both going to need you. When Terry opens his eyes — and he will, my dear, he will — the first face he sees must be yours.'

She was quieter now, her face hidden against him. Above the straight fair fall of her hair, his eyes met mine.

'Yes, I saw Terry today. I spoke to a new specialist there — and I'm delighted to say, Terry is showing some significant response at last! You realise what I'm saying, Benita?'

I understood. I whispered, 'Thank God.' There were no other words.

'So one day, he might give his own account of the accident, and finally clear your mind of any doubts.'

'That doesn't matter. So long as he recovers, that's all that matters!'

My voice broke. Almost it was too much to believe, that my nightmare of blackmail was past, but most of all that

Terry would live. In deepest relief and thankfulness, I accepted from Andrew a mumbled apology, just once looking into his pale, shamed face.

It was then that I was suddenly aware of Roger standing by my chair. He said quietly, 'You should have told me.' The hurt in those brief words came to me clearly.

'I know,' I whispered. 'I'm sorry.'

'I'm sorry too, that you didn't trust me enough to ask my help. But it's over now.' I felt his hand on my arm. 'We'll put these weeks behind us. You'll be leaving here. We've much happier things ahead of us.'

He didn't need to specify those. I was almost frightened to realise that all the burdens were lifted from my shoulders. I was through with Beacon House, a cause of discord between the two of us. My commitments to the Clinic had been honourably fulfilled, and there was nothing left to prevent my marriage to Roger.

But for the moment, those plans

must wait. Roger was concerned about returning promptly to London. On his way, he would drop Wendy safely back at her home.

She was still huddled on the settee, rather as though she would never move again. He asked her, 'Are you ready to leave, Mrs Stanton?'

'Yes, come on, Wendy,' I encouraged. 'Let Roger take you home. You need a nice long rest before you go to see Terry.'

I tried gently to raise the slumped figure. But Wendy gasped and clung to me.

'Please — please let me stay with you — ' Her voice was barely coherent. 'Help me, Dr Wilde, help me!'

All at once it was indeed the Dr Wilde of other times who bent over the sofa with quiet words and competent questioning hands. My only concern was for Wendy — and Wendy's baby, prematurely well on its way into the world. For hours through this traumatic day she had kept this secret, perhaps since the shock of two unexpected callers at her door this morning. Now, it could be kept secret no longer.

Vaguely, in the background, I heard Roger wondering whether to stay on, and Clive advising, 'No need, the lady knows what she's at.' Roger took him at his word with just a parting promise to ring later for news — and escorted Andrew Parker from the house as he left. There was no trouble about that. The young man was only too glad to escape.

'Well, don't just stand there like a spare part!' I looked round at Clive. 'Surely I don't have to tell you what's needed? I doubt if we've too much time . . . Tell Nurse Potter to come in here, and keep those noisy kids right out of the way!'

'Yes, ma'am,' Clive said meekly.

★ ★ ★

It was later that night when I left the local hospital. They had been long, difficult hours, but Wendy was sleeping now like an exhausted child. Her last waking words were a whispered question to me, 'Can I call him after you . . . 'Ben'? . . . I think Terry will like that . . . ' New-born Ben Stanton, frail but perfectly formed, was receiving every care.

I had travelled here by ambulance, and was more than pleased to find Clive's comfortably cluttered car waiting. When lights and houses were left behind, the headlights picked out a damp ribbon of road towards 'home'. Clive's home, never really mine.

'Come and sit by my fire for a nightcap,' he invited.

I was too tired to dissent. In his big office-sitting-room he turned up the fire to a comforting glow. Smiler was sprawled inelegantly among the usual mixture of crayons, jigsaws and official papers, watched by an impassive metal robot. Well, Clive Lowery would never change. But tomorrow, all of this would be just a bitter-sweet memory.

He passed a cup to me from the tray and muttering Elsie had just brought in 'Do you know, you've done a fine job all round today?'

I believed that was true. But I had to admit to myself, the credit for my renewed self-reliance that had carried me through was mostly due to him, and to his calculated risk of entrusting me with the Visitor's Day.

Ben's unscripted arrival was the moment when I found again a life-dream once abandoned in bitterness and despair. Only . . . was Roger a man to tolerate a wife less devoted to him than to her surgery desk and prescription pad? . . .

My eyelids drooping in the warmth, I had fallen into a deep reverie. But I roused at strange sounds in the corridor, scufflings and whispers. Clive whipped open the door to disclose a group of children in assorted nightwear, obviously trying in vain to find a spokesman.

'A midnight deputation?' he asked solemnly. 'All right, speak up, someone!'

'We heard Miss Wilde come in, see?' Jackie waded in. 'Well, you said she's going away tomorrow — '

'Indeed she is. A well-earned break with her folks in Devon.'

'Well, we want to know — is she coming back here afterwards?'

'Yes, we want her back!' others chimed in. But one voice made the plea more directly, as Kylie elbowed her way to the door, angrily scrubbing at her eyes. 'Miss, you will come back, won't you? You're not going there to live with them relatives permanent, Miss?'

I could only mumble, 'Don't worry, I-I'm sure I'll see you all again.' I was glad Clive was hustling the group back to their beds.

'Well?' Clive said. He returned to me, and quietly closed the door. 'And will you?'

'Of course, I'll drop by here some-time and — and say hello to everyone . . .'

Even as I spoke those stumbling words, I knew suddenly that very dearly I wanted to return here — and not just to 'drop by'. To resume an unfinished task, to return — at last the shattering truth stared me in the face — to Clive Lowery. Not the clinic's dedicated chief, but Clive the man.

I looked at him now as though a blindfold had dropped from my eyes. This man who had infuriated me with his obstinate opinions and the dazzle of a flamboyant personality so unlike my own, who had helped me find my own lost dream as no-one else could have helped, and in doing so had lighted up my life. Far, far off from the dear, deep friendship that I knew now was mine and Roger's, a precious, enduring friendship, nothing more . . .

'Which reminds me,' Clive said as though he had read those wild thoughts, and heaven forbid that he had! 'Here's a letter for you. Open it, don't mind me. I know the gist of it. When Roger left us and started off to London, he came back again soon after, but you'd left in the ambulance with Wendy so he sat down and wrote this for you.'

I read the lines of Roger's familiar handwriting over and over. A few stood out.

' . . . I've had doubts about your true interest in our future together, but watching you with Wendy today was a revelation, it's obvious your heart doesn't lie in the future I'd hoped for. It would be very selfish to hold you to a promise likely to endanger your happiness, so if it would help you to be free of our engagement . . . '

Silently, I looked across at the man watching me, the light gilding his greying fair hair, the freckled, quite unremarkable face unusually grave — until he smiled at me, the magic smile that churned my heart as I knew now it always had.

Indeed, it would be desperately unwise to return here, to be constantly near him! Now that I knew my true feelings, how could I possibly hide them? I muttered, 'Roger deserves a better wife than I'd ever be. But as for my job here, I don't think so.'

'No?'

'No. Oh, today was a success, but otherwise I've just disrupted all your work.' Painfully I plunged on. 'And I might still work things out with Roger. It would be cruel to walk out on him.'

'But — surely, far more cruel to live a life of pretence?'

I said shakily, 'You're very wise.'

'If I am, I wasn't always. This is my cue to tell you a story! You know the start already — or had you forgotten I was left abandoned at a hospital like a bundle of washing?'

'How could I forget that!'

'But maybe you thought everything after was all sweetness and light? It wasn't! A lot of well-meaning, hard-working people, foster parents, children's homes, child psychiatrists — they wore themselves out trying to help. I was labelled a rebel against any kind of authority.

'By the time I was as old as the Welles boys here, or Paul, or Mandy Holt

— I'd been excluded from a couple of schools and was pretty well known at the local. Did it ever cross your mind that the boss of a centre for budding young delinquents might have a record himself?'

Certainly I had not guessed. I whispered, 'Clive, I'm beginning to see why you understand our children here so well. You're not going to tell me you ended up —?'

'In prison? Not quite. When I was trying to abscond, yet again, from this special youth rehab unit, I fell off a roof into a yard. It was a high roof, and a hard concrete yard. Well, I was in hospital for an age, and I came under the care of an odd little man, Dr Josef Colouris — a pointed beard and an accent you could cut with a knife, no-one took him seriously. He used what was left of me as a guinea pig for his pet theories. I was a captive audience, you don't run far with an injured spine and two smashed legs — I thought it grossly unfair at the time!'

I just gazed at him.

'It took a long while, but he got through to me,' he went quietly on. 'He used to say, broken bodies would mend, but the sickness of self-pity and hatred I'd fallen into was far harder to heal. Gradually, he convinced me it wasn't too late to make a new start. When the urge came to me to study medicine, he encouraged me all the way. It was so sad that he died a couple of years later — but I was sure there must be ways to develop his basic ideas. For a long time it's been my dream to start up a place where naughty kids on the downward path could be helped before it's too late . . .'

A tap on the door disturbed a deep, thinking hush that fell on the room. 'Another insomniac? Well, this place gets to us all in the end. Come in and join us, Sharon!' Clive invited her cordially.

★ ★ ★

It was a typed envelope Sharon laid on the desk before him. Her attractive, dark-eyed face was pale, but she was very composed.

'I won't stay, thank you. I don't want to disturb you, I — just wanted to give you this. A fortnight's notice,' she said bleakly, 'but I'd rather leave right away, if you don't mind.'

'You know I mind. Listen, please take it back. You're needed here, my dear. Think about it some more.'

'No!' Sharon said sharply. Clearly, it would take very little to make her break down. 'My uncle is buying a hotel, he wants me to manage it. I told him, 'yes'.

She glanced not once at me, nor at the letter he was still offering her back. She almost ran from the room, from the presence of the man she had so idolised.

'Clive, go after her!' I urged him.

He shook his head. 'It's better she goes. A clean break, a fresh start. Oh, I've always been very fond of her, only that wasn't enough . . . ' His eyes

191

looked suddenly straight into mine. 'Especially after I met you.'

I gazed back at him. My ears had heard, but my mind didn't believe.

'Didn't you know I love you?' he asked simply. 'Sharon knew. Roger knew.'

'But — but — ' My voice came out strained and shocked. 'You hardly know me, I've been here only weeks — only days!'

'What does time have to do with it? It's feelings that matter, not days, years . . . ' I realised he was kneeling at my feet on the worn office carpet. I wasn't sure if Smiler or myself were more utterly amazed. 'You know I've no family estate to offer you, just a make-believe name and some credit card debts, but instead I offer the devotion of my most adoring heart. I truly love you, more than I can ever tell you . . . '

I was wide awake, fully conscious. It was no dream. I said faintly, 'Good grief!' 'Miss Wilde,' he remonstrated, 'have you no romance in your soul? Come on. Will you consider marrying me?'

It was a sudden burst of laughter from the doorway that made Clive jump to his feet, his question still unanswered. The door was ajar after Sharon's flight, and in the gap were framed three or four mirthful faces. The children were finding this quite a carnival night.

As Clive started towards them with apparent severity, the boys fled. He went a little way in pursuit, sending them scuttling upstairs. I heard him chasing after them with dire threats of extra maths with Mrs Peake.

Though he wasn't absent long, it gave me a moment to collect my whirling thoughts. I needed it. When he returned to me, a little red in the face and short of breath, I was ready with an outpouring of words.

'We'll look after my grandfather, won't we? I'll phone him first thing in the morning, I know he'll be thrilled

— he liked you a lot even though he thought you were a little bit crazy! And listen, I know this isn't the time to think of it, but — if we extend Beacon House, get more staff, how would you feel about working with children who've suffered personality changes due to illness or injury? I once had a most interesting case — '

'Excuse me,' he requested mildly. 'Does this mean your answer is 'yes'?'

'Eh? Oh! Of course, it's 'yes, please!' — you're such an expert mind-reader, you've probably known I love you long before I found out myself! And Clive, how would you feel about us being long-term foster parents to Kylie? Or considering adoption? She's special, she really brought us together and we could do so much for her. And don't you think we could make a fine man of poor dear Frankie if we took him on as well?'

'Hold on.' He made an exaggerated gesture of wiping his brow. 'You're a glutton for punishment, aren't you?

Never mind, whatever Dr Wilde pre-scribes for our future is fine with me.'

'*Our* future . . . ' I echoed, and suddenly was quiet at the sound of the words.

'Ours, Kylie's, Frankie's — maybe more along the way, who knows? But just for now, why are we wasting time talking about it?'

He made sure we wasted no more. His arms held me close in engulfing warmth. His lips on mine were strong and tender, a kiss to drive all else from my mind.

'I love you, Bennie,' he whispered.

THE END

We do hope that you have enjoyed reading this large print book.

Did you know that all of our titles are available for purchase?

We publish a wide range of high quality large print books including:
Romances, Mysteries, Classics
General Fiction
Non Fiction and Westerns

Special interest titles available in large print are:
The Little Oxford Dictionary
Music Book, Song Book
Hymn Book, Service Book

Also available from us courtesy of Oxford University Press:
Young Readers' Dictionary
(large print edition)
Young Readers' Thesaurus
(large print edition)

For further information or a free brochure, please contact us at:
Ulverscroft Large Print Books Ltd.,
The Green, Bradgate Road, Anstey,
Leicester, LE7 7FU, England.
Tel: (00 44) **0116 236 4325**
Fax: (00 44) **0116 234 0205**

HER HEART'S DESIRE

Dorothy Taylor

When Beth Garland's great aunt Emily dies, she leaves Greg, her boyfriend, in Manchester — along with her successful advertising job — to return to live in Emily's cottage. Feeling disillusioned with Greg and his high-handed attitude, she finds herself more and more attracted to her aunt's gardener, Noah. But Noah seems to be hiding from the past, whilst Greg has his own ideas about the direction of their relationship. Surrounded by secrecy and deceit, how will Beth ever find true love?

PRECIOUS MOMENTS

June Gadsby

The heartbreak was all behind her, but hearing her name mentioned on the radio, and that song — their special song — brought bittersweet memories rushing back through the years. It had to be a coincidence, and was best forgotten — but then Lara opened the door to find her past standing there. The moment of truth she had dreaded for years had finally arrived, and she wasn't sure how to handle it . . .

THE SECRET OF SHEARWATER

Diney Delancey

When Zoe Carson inherits a cottage in Cornwall, she takes a holiday from her job in London to stay at the cottage. There, she makes friends with the local people, including the hot-tempered Gregory Enodoc. Zoe is glad of their friendship when events take a sinister turn and the police become involved. And when she decides to leave London to live permanently at the cottage, Zoe is unaware of the dangers into which this will lead her . . .

SWEET CHALLENGE

Joyce Johnson

London life for Chloe Duncan is changed forever when she accepts an invitation to visit her previously unknown Scottish great aunt, Flora Duncan. Chloe loves the peace and beauty of rural Highland life at Flora's croft, but mysteries and tensions in her great aunt's past disturb this tranquillity. Land disputes involve her in danger and, whilst unravelling the mystery of Flora's lost love, Chloe's own heart is jeopardised when she meets handsome New Zealander Steve McGlarran . . .

OBERON'S CHILD

Valerie Holmes

Faith is wilful and beautiful and loves her mother, Prudence, dearly. However, she hates the man she calls 'Father'. Oberon Wild is a proud, overbearing man who succeeded in making a fortune through his mill, but who failed at the one thing he wanted more than anything — to sire a son and heir. How then will Faith escape from an unwanted engagement, protect her mother from Oberon's wrath and ultimately be with Benjamin, the man she loves?

ROMANY ROSE

nts
er
a-
ar
ng
ed
ro.
nd
m
ut
as
he
ue